Heather from Nannie.
Christmas 1960.

THE BOBBSEY TWINS
IN THE COUNTRY

"Here he comes!" the boys called as the big parachute
floated down

The Bobbsey Twins in the Country

By

LAURA LEE HOPE

Published by

WORLD DISTRIBUTORS (MANCHESTER) LIMITED

LONDON – MANCHESTER

ENGLAND

THE BOBBSEY TWINS BOOKS
By Laura Lee Hope

First impression 1955
Reprinted 1955
Reprinted 1956
Reprinted 1957
Reprinted 1958

CONTENTS

CHAPTER I

AN EXCITING INVITATION

"THERE'S the door bell! It's the postman. I'll go!" Freddie exclaimed.

He and his twin sister Flossie had been waiting for Mr. Garret, the postman, to arrive, because an important letter was coming.

"Oh, let me! It's my turn today!" cried Flossie.

"I see a blue envelope!" her brother said excitedly. "It's the right letter! Aunt Sarah always writes on blue paper!"

Flossie and Freddie had been taking turns meeting Mr. Garret for the past few days. Their mother had said she was looking for a letter from Aunt Sarah.

Each child was making a great effort to reach the front door first. Freddie won by jumping over a low table that stood in his way.

"I beat you," laughed the little boy.

"Hallo," smiled the postman, handing the

mail to Freddie. "Hope your important letter is here."

"This is it," said Freddie, tapping the blue envelope.

"Mummy's in the sewing-room," said Flossie. "Come on, Freddie."

The two climbed the stairs, with the welcome letter from Aunt Sarah clutched tightly in Freddie's fist.

Freddie and Flossie were the younger of the two pairs of Bobbsey twins. They had been to kindergarten. Both were chubby, and very cute, with blond curly hair and dimpled faces. The older Bobbsey twins, Nan and Bert, were nearly six years older; dark, handsome, and as alike as "two peas in a pod", the neighbours always said.

"What does Aunt Sarah say?" broke in Freddie, as his mother read the letter to herself. He was hoping it would be an invitation to visit Meadow Brook, the farm where Aunt Sarah and Uncle Daniel lived.

"Now be patient," Mrs. Bobbsey told him. "I'll read her letter to you in just a minute."

The twins could hardly keep still. They watched her face intently and could tell from the twinkle in her eyes that the letter contained something very interesting.

"Aunt Sarah asks how we all are," Mrs. Bobbsey finally said.

"Oh, we're all fine," Freddie interrupted impatiently.

"Please listen, Freddie, or we won't hear," Flossie begged, tugging at his elbow to keep him from jumping around.

"Then she says," continued Mrs. Bobbsey, "that this is a beautiful summer at Meadow Brook."

"Course it is. We know that!" broke in Freddie again.

"Freddie!" exclaimed Flossie.

"And she asks how would we like to visit her and Uncle Daniel this summer?"

"Fine. Like it—lovely!" the little boy shouted, getting his words mixed up in his delight. "Mother, tell her we'll come. Send her a letter quick!"

"Freddie Bobbsey!" spoke up Flossie. "If you would only keep quiet, we could hear about going."

"Well, I was only saying——" pouted Freddie.

"Now listen." Their mother went on reading from the letter, "Aunt Sarah says Cousin Harry can hardly wait until holiday time to see Bert, and she also says, 'How I want a hug from those small twins!'"

"Good! Goody!" broke in the irrepressible Freddie again. "I'll hug Aunt Sarah just like this," and he grabbed his mother around the neck and squeezed her until she begged him to stop.

"I guess she'll like that," Freddie boasted.

"Not if you mess up her hair," Flossie insisted, while their mother fixed her hair and straightened her collar, all the while laughing.

"Is that all?" Flossie asked.

"No, there is a message for Bert and Nan too, but I must keep that until lunch-time. Nobody likes stale news," Mrs. Bobbsey replied.

"But can't we hear it when Bert and Nan come home?" coaxed Flossie.

"Of course," her mother assured her. "But now you two run outdoors and play."

"Oh, aren't you glad!" exclaimed Flossie to her brother, as they ran outside and along the stone wall that edged the pretty terrace in front of their home.

"Glad! I'm just—so glad—so glad—I could almost fly up in the air!"

The morning passed quickly for the little twins. When their brother and sister appeared round the corner, Flossie and Freddie hurried to meet them.

"We're going! We're going!" was all Freddie could say.

"It's in a letter. There's a surprise for you. It's Meadow Brook," was Flossie's way of telling the news.

At the lunch table Mrs. Bobbsey finished the letter. "'Tell Nan,'" she read, "'that I have found a new kind of chocolate candy that I am going to teach her to make.' There, Nan, you see," commented Mrs. Bobbsey, "Aunt Sarah has not forgotten what a good little cook you are."

"Chocolate candy," remarked Bert, and smacked his lips. "Say, Nan, be sure to make a lot. It sounds good."

Just then Dinah, the cook, brought in the dessert, which was a big lemon meringue pie, and the children tried to tell her about going to the country. But so many were talking at once that the plump, good-natured negro woman could only laugh.

"Yes, Dinah," Mrs. Bobbsey told her, "we're going to the country, and listen to Aunt Sarah's message to you."

Once more the blue letter came out, and Mrs. Bobbsey read:

"'Be sure to bring Dinah! We have plenty of room, and she will so enjoy seeing the farm.'"

"Farm! That I do like," Dinah replied. "Used to farm all the time down home in Virginia! Yes, Dinah'll go and hoe the corn and——" Turning to Bert, she grinned. "Are there any water-melons at Meadow Brook? You and I——"

Dinah stopped talking.

The Bobbseys looked at one another, wondering what Dinah had in mind. When she did not tell them, Bert spoke up.

"You and I what?" he asked.

CHAPTER II

THE MUSIC MACHINE

DINAH looked at Mrs. Bobbsey, then at Bert.

"Well, I was a-figurin'," the cook laughed, "that maybe Bert and old Dinah could have a water-melon-eatin' contest. But maybe we'd better not. Bert might get himself sick!"

"How about you?" Nan teased.

"Oh, I could eat water-melon till the cows come home," declared Dinah, as she went chuckling to the kitchen.

The others laughed, too, then started talking excitedly again about going to Meadow Brook Farm. They would be leaving Lakeport in just two weeks!

As you may remember, the twins and their parents lived in a comfortable house in Lakeport, where Mr. Bobbsey was in the lumber business. Mr. and Mrs. Bobbsey were young in spirit, and always took part in their children's joys and sorrows, for there were sorrows sometimes.

Once poor little Freddie got shut up all alone in a big store with only a little black kitten named Snoop to keep him from being too scared.

Freddie had gone shopping one day with his mother, and wandered off. Finally he fell asleep in a storage room. The store closed and he was locked in! When he awoke, it was dark, and when the great big janitor came to rescue him—oh! Freddie thought the man was a giant with his great deep voice.

Freddie often got into trouble, but like most bright boys he was always saved just at the right time.

Nan, Bert, and Flossie all had plenty of exciting experiences too, some of them caused by that bully, Danny Rugg, a boy Bert's age, who always tried to make trouble for Bert, and sometimes succeeded.

Of course, Nan had lots of friends, as all girls have, but Bert was really her closest companion, just as Freddie was Flossie's.

"When we get to the country we can swim and hike and go picnicking," Nan said one day.

"Yes, and I'm going out exploring with Harry," announced Bert.

"I'm just going to plant things," Flossie declared quaintly. "I just love beans and ice-cream and——"

"Ice-cream! You can't plant ice-cream!" Freddie interrupted.

The others laughed, and Bert said it certainly would be swell if you could.

"I'm going to have chickens," Freddie told them. "I'm going to have one of those funny chicken coops that you shut up tight and then when you open it, it's full of cheep-cheeps."

"Oh, an incubator, you mean," Nan explained. "That's a nice warm house for baby chickens that haven't any mother."

"But mine are going to have a mother," Freddie corrected, thinking how sad little chicks would be without a mother as kind as his own.

"But how can they have a mother when there isn't any for them?" Flossie asked.

"I'll get them one," Freddie protested. "I'll let Snoop be their mummy."

"A cat! The idea! Why, he'd eat 'em all up," Flossie argued.

"Not if I spank him for doing it," her twin insisted.

Nan and Bert laughed.

"What is the good of spanking the kitten after the chickens are all eaten up?" asked Nan.

So the merry days went on until at last holiday time came!

"Just one more night," Nan told Flossie, as she watched her little sister get ready for bed.

Bert was assisting his mother with the packing, for taking the whole Bobbsey family to the country meant lots of clothes, besides some books and dolls and toys. Then there was Bert's tool-box that he was so proud of. He might need that at Meadow Brook. Even Snoop was going along.

Morning came at last. It was a beautiful bright day, a rare one for travelling. A hard shower the evening before had washed and cooled the country-side.

"Come now, children," Mr. Bobbsey told the excited youngsters. "Keep track of your things. Sam will be ready in a few minutes, and then we must be off."

Promptly Sam, who was Dinah's husband and worked for Mr. Bobbsey, drove up to the door with the family's big car, and the children hurried to get in. They were just ready to start when Freddie cried out:

"Oh, Snoop, Snoop! He's in the living-room in his basket! Please let me get him!" and he ran back after the kitten.

They had driven only a short way when Dinah exclaimed, "Oh, my goodness! The lunch!" She explained that she had left a box of sandwiches on the kitchen table.

"Never mind, we'll eat when we get to the farm," said Mrs. Bobbsey.

Dinah shook her head sadly. "Nobody can cook ham like your Dinah, Mis' Bobbsey. And I'm sure these here twins are goin' to get hungry in an hour. They hardly ate any breakfast!"

"That's right," said Mr. Bobbsey. "And we shan't get to Meadow Brook until one o'clock. When we reach the station, Sam had better go home and get the sandwiches. I think he can make it before our train comes."

The railway station was reached without anything more being forgotten. While Mr. Bobbsey attended to having the luggage checked at the window in the waiting-room, Sam drove home as fast as was safe in the traffic.

The children walked about, exploring. Freddie let Flossie hold Snoop in his covered basket. Suddenly an express train thundered through the station. The kitten was so scared he gave a jump that knocked the basket right out of the little girl's arms.

"Oh, oh, you poor kitty!" cried Flossie. "Are you hurt?"

She opened the basket and lifted Snoop out.

The kitten snuggled in her arms and seemed to be unhurt.

Meanwhile, Freddie had gone back into the waiting-room. He was standing by Dinah, staring at a strange sight. A stout lady was standing on a little platform near by, and music was playing.

"What is it?" Freddie asked.

"That's a weighing machine," Dinah said with a laugh. "You just put a penny in it and it tells you how much you weigh, besides playin' a tune."

The stout lady got off. Freddie tugged at Dinah's hand.

"I want to hear some more music," he said. "You get on. You're fat." Freddie thought the weighing machine just worked for stout people.

Good-natured Dinah took a penny from her purse and Freddie put it in the slot. Dinah looked a little scared as the indicator nearly reached fifteen stone, but when she heard the soft strains of an old Virginia melody, she started to hum softly.

"Now, isn't this fine!" she exclaimed. "Wouldn't it be wonderful to have a music-box weighing machine in our house?" Freddie agreed that it would.

The interesting sights in the railway station had to be given up now, for a voice called through a loudspeaker:

"All aboard for Meadow Brook!" and the Bobbseys hurried to the platform.

As Freddie was hustled toward the platform, holding his mother's hand, he suddenly stopped.

"We must hurry, Freddie," Mrs. Bobbsey said, urging him toward the waiting train.

"But, Mummy," he cried, "Sam hasn't come back with our sandwiches!"

CHAPTER III

SNOOP GETS AWAY

"ALL aboard!" the guard called.

Suddenly Freddie cried out, "Here he comes! Please don't let the train go!"

The guard smiled as Sam came racing up and handed the box of sandwiches to Dinah. Then he waved good-bye again.

The Bobbseys got aboard and went into a carriage with big soft seats.

"Mother, the seats go around," said Freddie excitedly.

He was already planning how he could ride around and around in them. But a smiling porter said:

"Follow me, little boy."

He led the small twins and Dinah, who was carrying Snoop as well as the box of sandwiches, to a little room at the end of the carriage. There were two long seats in it facing each other. As he shut the door, the porter said, grinning:

"Your daddy was wise to get this compartment for you children. You won't have to sit still in here. You can play games and have a lot of fun."

Freddie forgot about the chairs that went around and around, even though his mother and father and Bert and Nan were sitting in some just outside.

"I'm going to let Snoop out," said Freddie.

He opened the basket. The kitten got up, stretched, and jumped out. Just then Mr. Bobbsey opened the door. Snoop scooted out into the chair car and perched himself on a nearby window sill to look out at the scenery whirling past.

"Oh!" exclaimed Mrs. Bobbsey. The guard will put him off the train!" She tried to catch the now happy little kitten, but he jumped to the floor and went under a chair.

"Here, Snoop," coaxed Nan, also alarmed. "Come, Snoop!"

But the kitten had been a captive long enough to appreciate his liberty now. So he refused to be coaxed. Flossie came along between the chairs very cautiously, and stooped down. As soon as Snoop saw her arm stretch out for him, he ran up the carriage. Then suddenly he leaped to the back of a seat.

Bert had dashed up the coach. As he made a

dive for Snoop, the kitten bounded over the head of a lady sleeping in the chair. He landed right in her lap!

"Oh, mercy me!" screamed the lady, as she awoke with Snoop's tail whisking over her face. "Goodness, gracious! What is that?"

Before she realized it was only a kitten on her lap, she jumped up on the seat, and looked just like the funny pictures of a woman afraid of a mouse. The people around could not help laughing, but Freddie and the other Bobbseys were frightened.

"Oh, will they take Snoop away?" Freddie asked. He was almost crying.

By this time the frightened lady had found out it was only a little kitten. Feeling very foolish, she sat down and tried to coax Snoop into her lap again. But Snoop ran under another chair.

Mr. Bobbsey hurried to apologize and get the cat. "We'll have to put Snoop back in his basket," he declared.

But that was easier said than done, for no sooner would one of the Bobbseys approach the cat than Snoop would hide in a new place.

At this moment the guard came in from the next coach. Freddie felt as he if could not breathe, he was so frightened, and tears ran down Flossie's cheeks.

"Will he put Snoop off the train?" Freddie blubbered, thinking of every horrible story he had ever heard. Mr. Bobbsey, too, was a little bit alarmed.

Now Snoop was a very bright little kitten. When he saw the guard coming, he made up his mind that the right thing to do would be to make friends with him. When the guard stooped to catch the offending kitten, Snoop walked right up to him, sniffed his uniform, and stepped up on the man's outstretched hand.

"Well, you are a nice little kitty," the guard admitted, fondling Snoop in spite of orders.

"Oh, please, Mr. Guard, give me my cat!" cried Freddie.

"Yours, is it? Well, I don't blame you for bringing this cat along. Say," and the man leaned down to the frightened Freddie, "it's against orders, but I'd just like to take this kitten to the kitchen and treat him to a piece of fish. I declare he's—he's the cutest kitten I've ever seen!" And the guard fondled Snoop until he purred contentedly.

Freddie and the other Bobbsey twins were relieved to know that only something nice was going to happen to Snoop. All of them wanted to see the kitchen on the train, so they followed the nice guard.

Everybody along the aisle wanted to pet Snoop, who from starting as a little stowaway had now become a hero. More than once Freddie and Flossie stumbled against the sides of the big seats as the train rushed along with breath-taking speed, but each time Nan or Bert caught them. At last, after passing through the big dining car, they reached the kitchen.

"What you got there? Something for my soup?" asked the good-natured cook, who was really very fond of cats.

"Oh, no!" exclaimed Freddie, looking up pleadingly at the kind guard. Then when he saw both men grinning he knew the cook was only joking.

The guard explained that he wanted to give Snoop something to eat.

"Sure enough," said the cook.

Snoop drank a saucer of milk like a little gentleman.

"That's the way to drink on a fast train," laughed the guard. "Then you don't spill it on your clothes!"

The dainty kitten took two other courses, one of a little fish and one of a titbit of meat, in splendid traveller fashion.

Seeing the kitten eat made the Bobbsey twins very hungry. Suddenly they remembered the sandwiches Dinah had brought.

Freddie started to run back to Dinah, but he fell down in the dining car and bumped his head. He was glad to take Nan's hand after that. Flossie held Bert's. When they reached the little compartment, they put Snoop in his basket.

"You can't have any more 'ventures," Flossie told him, closing the lid.

The kitten did not seem to mind. He curled up and fell asleep. The four children each ate a ham sandwich, and Nan brought in cups of water from the end of the carriage.

The train was speeding along with that regular motion which makes many travellers drowsy. Freddie watched the scenery for a time. Then the click of the wheels on the rails made him sleepy, and soon he curled up on the seat and closed his eyes.

"Poor little fellow!" Dinah remarked. "He's all worn out from worryin' about Snoop!"

Flossie's pretty dimpled face was pressed close to the window-pane. She was admiring the big world that seemed to be running away from the train. But soon she grew tired of it.

"It seems as if we've been on the train all day," the little girl sighed.

"In another hour we'll be there," said Dinah kindly. "Suppose you take a nap, too. Then you'll feel real good when we get to Meadow Brook."

It was easy to follow this suggestion, and the next thing Flossie and Freddie knew, Daddy and Mummy and Dinah were waking them up to leave the train.

"Now, don't forget anything," Mr. Bobbsey cautioned his family, as hats and coats were put on and parcels picked up.

Freddie was still very sleepy, and his daddy had to shake him a little, while the others, with some excitement, hurried on ahead. When they were standing on the platform, and the train was starting off, Freddie suddenly cried out:

"Oh, Snoop, Snoop! I forgot Snoop! Get him quick!"

CHAPTER IV

A FRISKY CALF

"THAT little old kitten again!" Dinah exclaimed. "He's more trouble than—than the whole family!"

Gradually the train picked up speed, and it seemed as if Snoop was gone this time for sure.

"Snoop!" cried Freddie in dismay.

Just then the kind guard who had shut the door and gone inside the train, suddenly appeared at the carriage door with the basket in his hand. Quickly he opened the top half of the door.

When Bert saw him, he started running alongside the moving train. The guard reached out and the boy grabbed the basket. Bert shouted his thanks as the train rumbled off.

"Goody! Goody!" shouted Flossie and Freddie together.

"Well, I declare, such excitement!" said a good-natured little lady, trying to surround all the Bobbseys at once.

27

"Aunt Sarah!" exclaimed the children.

"Uncle Dan!"

"Harry!"

"Hallo! Hallo! How are you?" Such kissing and hand-shaking had not been seen by the elderly ticket collector at the Meadow Brook Station for some time.

"Here at last!" Uncle Daniel declared, grabbing up Freddie and giving him the kind of hug Freddie had intended for Aunt Sarah.

The big station wagon from Uncle Daniel Bobbsey's farm stood behind the station. Into this the Bobbseys piled, bag and baggage, not forgetting the little black cat.

"All aboard for Meadow Brook Farm!" called Uncle Dan, as he drove the car down the shady country road.

"Oh, how beautiful the trees are out here!" Nan exclaimed, as they sped along. They were so close to the low trees that she could have reached out and picked off some of the leaves.

"It smells mighty sweet!" said Dinah, as she sniffed, enjoying the freshness of the country air.

Freddie was on the front seat with Uncle Dan and had Snoop's basket safe in his arms. He wanted to let the kitten out to enjoy the scenery along the road, but everybody protested.

"No more Snoop trouble this trip," laughed

Mr. Bobbsey. "He has had all the fun he needs for today." So Freddie had to be content.

At each farm along the way to Meadow Brook Farm, children called out to Harry, who had told them his cousins were coming.

"Here we are," called Uncle Daniel, as they turned into the neat gravel driveway leading to a rambling farm-house. On each side of the drive grew straight lines of boxwood, and around the house were well-kept beds of beautiful flowers.

"Oh, don't you love them, Mother?" Nan asked.

Mrs. Bobbsey smiled and nodded. As Uncle Dan stopped in front of the broad white porch, an elderly woman came out the door.

"Hallo, Martha!" called the visitors, as the faithful old servant smiled a welcome. She was not coloured like Dinah, but looked as if she were just as full of fun as the Bobbseys' cook.

"Got here at last!" she exclaimed. "You must be starved."

"Glad to see you, Martha," Dinah told her. "You see, I had to come along to help you with such a lot of folks. And we brought a new member of the family, our kitty Snoop."

"The more the merrier," replied Martha. "One more pet at Meadow Brook won't matter. We have lots of 'em."

"I'm starved to death!" Mr. Bobbsey laughed, as the aroma of a fine dinner reached him.

"We'll clean up a bit and come right to the table," Mrs. Bobbsey added.

Soon after this all the Bobbseys, Richard's family and Daniel's family, gathered in the long, old-fashioned dining-room. They were served one of the finest meals they had ever eaten, the twins' mother declared.

"You must have creamy cows here," said Flossie, looking at her glass of rich milk.

Uncle Dan's eyes twinkled. "Now the cow that gave that milk is brown, Flossie. How do you figure that out?" he teased.

Bert, who was sitting next to Flossie, whispered to her, "Tell him you'll ask the cow!"

Dinner was very merry. When it was over, the baggage was opened, and holiday clothes were put on. Bert was ready first, and soon he and Harry were running down the road to meet the other boys and make plans for a picnic.

Meanwhile Nan had gone with her uncle Daniel, who wanted to show her his flower gardens. Nan learned that behind the farmhouse were very large gardens, from which her uncle sometimes sold flowers.

"I pride myself on my zinnias especially," he said, pointing. "I start 'em in my greenhouse.

Just see those yellows, and those pinks. Some are as big as pancakes."

"They are just beautiful, Uncle Dan," Nan replied in real admiration. "I love zinnias. They bloom so long."

"All summer. Now, what do you think of my sweet peas?" he asked, walking over to where the flowers were growing in long rows on wire netting.

"They're giants!" said Nan. She had never seen such tall, sturdy stems and such huge flowers, and how heavenly they smelled!

She and Uncle Daniel went from one flower-bed to another, and Nan thought never before had she seen such beautiful roses and larkspur.

Flossie and Freddie were out near the chicken coop with Aunt Sarah. She had given each of them a handful of corn to scatter to the hens.

"Oh, Auntie, what funny little chickens!" Flossie exclaimed, pointing to a couple of strutting birds that were eagerly eating corn with the chickens.

"Those are Harry's homing pigeons," her aunt explained. "Someday we must go off to the woods and let the birds fly home with a letter to Dinah and Martha."

"What do you mean?" Flossie asked.

Aunt Sarah explained that homing pigeons

can be taken miles and miles and miles away
from where they live, and still find their way
back home.

"For this reason they are sometimes used to
carry messages," she said. "A tiny letter is tied
to the pigeon's leg."

"Oh, please let's do it right now," Freddie
urged.

"Not today, dear," Aunt Sarah told him.
"These are Harry's pigeons, and you should play
that game with him. Come, let me show you
Frisky, our new little calf."

"Could I ride her?" Freddie asked, as they
opened the barnyard gate and went in.

"A calf isn't for riding," said Flossie. "That's
only horses."

Frisky the calf was tied to a stake in the barnyard. As they went up to her, she rubbed her head
affectionately against Aunt Sarah's skirt.

"Let me take her for a walk," Freddie asked.

"Calves don't walk either," Flossie persisted,
remembering pictures in her story-books. "They
mostly run."

"I could just hold the rope, couldn't I, Aunt
Sarah?" Freddie pleaded.

Aunt Sarah laughed, and said she guessed that
would be all right. She walked into the barn to
show Flossie the horses.

Now Freddie did not mean to do anything wrong. And, of course, he had no idea that Frisky was going to do what she did. Freddie told himself that it would not hurt to take the pretty little calf for a walk around the barnyard, so he took the rope off the stake and put the loop around his right wrist.

"Come, Frisky, take a walk," suggested Freddie, and quite obediently the calf walked along.

But suddenly Frisky spied the open gate and the lovely green grass outside. Without the slightest warning, the calf threw her hind legs up in the air, then bolted straight for the gate, dragging Freddie along after her.

CHAPTER V

STRANGE SOUNDS

"WHOA, Frisky! Whoa!" yelled Freddie, but the calf paid no attention.

Hearing Freddie's cry, Aunt Sarah and Flossie rushed from the barn.

"Oh, my goodness!" exclaimed Aunt Sarah.

"Whoa, whoa!" the little boy kept yelling, but he might as well have called giddap, for Frisky was going so fast now that poor little Freddie was being bumped and bruised as he was pulled along the ground.

"Look out, Freddie! Let go!" called Aunt Sarah as she saw Frisky heading for an apple tree.

But Freddie could not let go. The next instant Frisky made a dash around the tree, once, then again, winding the rope as she went, and brushing Freddie against the side of the tree.

"Oh!" Freddie moaned.

34

At that very moment the rope slipped over the calf's head and she skittered happily away.

"Are you dead?" cried Flossie, running up.

"Oh!" moaned the boy again, as Aunt Sarah bent over him. "Please—please catch—Frisky!"

"Never mind her," Aunt Sarah said anxiously. "Are you hurt, dear?"

"No," Freddie insisted. He knew anything that had happened to him was only punishment that he deserved.

"Your poor arm!" Flossie gasped. "It's all cut!"

"Firemen get hurt sometimes," Freddie spoke up. "And I'm going to be a fireman. I was like one that time, 'cause I tried to save somebody and didn't care if I got hurt!"

"You are a brave little boy," Aunt Sarah assured him. "You go and wash your arm good and clean, while I try to get that crazy Frisky."

By this time the calf was well on her way to the vegetable garden, where many delicious things to eat were growing. At that very moment Bert and Harry and two other boys turned in at the driveway.

"Runaway calf! Runaway calf!" called Harry. "Stop the runaway! Head her off!" Instantly all the boys started in pursuit.

But Frisky could run faster. Besides, she had

the advantage of a good start, and now she dashed along as if the whole affair were the biggest joke ever. She raced through the vegetable garden, and headed for a thicket some distance beyond. In a moment she disappeared.

"The river! The river!" cried Harry. "She'll jump in!"

As the boys squeezed in and out among the bushes near the water, Frisky plunged along through the dense shrubbery. Suddenly there was the sound of a splash. Frisky must be in the river!

"Oh, she's gone now, sure!" called Harry.

It took some time for the boys to reach the spot where they had heard the splash. The calf was not in sight.

"Where is she?" Harry asked, worried.

"There are her hoofprints!" Bert shouted, pointing.

"And they end here!" Harry added, indicating the very brink of the river.

"Frisky's gone!"

"But how could she drown so quickly?" Bert asked.

"Guess she went down in the channel," Tom Mason, one of the boys, answered soberly.

"Listen! Thought I heard something in the bushes," Bert whispered.

But no welcome sound came to tell them that poor Frisky was hiding in the brushwood. With heavy hearts the boys finally turned away.

They did not even feel like talking, somehow. They had counted on bringing the calf back in triumph.

When Flossie and Freddie saw them come back without Frisky, they both burst into tears and no one could stop their crying.

"I made her get drowned!" Freddie blubbered.

"Now maybe Frisky didn't go into the water after all," said Aunt Sarah soothingly.

But as the afternoon wore on and there was no news of Frisky, though everyone kept on looking, Freddie almost became ill. He said he did not want any supper.

"Never you mind, Freddie," Dinah told him. "Dinah'll go and fetch that Frisky back tomorrow. See if she don't. You just don't worry no more, but eat your supper and take a good sleep, 'cause we're goin' to have a picnic tomorrow, don't you remember?"

The others tried to comfort the little boy too, and Uncle Daniel said he knew where he could buy another calf just like Frisky, so after a while Freddie felt better. He even laughed when Martha made the white cat Fluffy play ball with Snoop in the big, low-ceilinged kitchen.

Then bedtime came and the eventful day finally closed for the Bobbseys.

"I wonder if something else will happen tonight," Bert remarked to Harry as they were undressing for bed.

"It's early yet," said Harry. "There's plenty of time. And Dad always says it's never late here until it's time to get early again!"

"Sounds so strange to hear—those—those——" Bert had tumbled into bed and was getting drowsy.

"Crickets," Harry told him, "and tree toads and katydids. Oh, there's lots to listen to if you don't get too sleepy."

The house soon became quiet, for even the grown-ups had gone to bed. Suddenly there was the sound of footsteps in the driveway. The next minute someone called out in the night:

"Hallo there! All asleep! Wake up, somebody!"

Freddie was the first to wake up and ran into his mother's and father's room.

"Come down here, Daniel!" the voice continued.

"Oh, is that you, Peter?" Uncle Daniel called out of the window. "I'll be right down," and soon afterwards appeared on the front porch.

"What do you think of this?" Mr. Burns asked.

"Well, I declare!" Uncle Daniel exclaimed, loud enough for all the listeners at the windows to hear. "So you've got Frisky? Well, I'm very glad indeed. Especially on Freddie's account. Where did you find her?"

"I went in my barn a while ago with a lantern," explained Peter Burns, "and if there wasn't a strange calf asleep with mine as cosy as could be!"

Mr. Burns said he wondered where in the world it had come from. When he got back to the house, his wife told him one was missing from Meadow Brook Farm.

"I brought her over tonight for fear you might miss her and get to lookin'," the farmer explained. "Otherwise I wouldn't have disturbed you."

By this time Uncle Daniel's hired man was up too, and offered to take Frisky back to her own bed in the barn—but not until Freddie had clattered downstairs and outdoors to make sure the calf really was Frisky and was all right.

"Oh, you're back! You're back!" he cried, hugging Frisky tightly. "I'll never let you loose again."

Freddie wanted to help put the playful animal to bed, but Uncle Daniel said the little boy should get back upstairs at once to his own bed. As Freddie crawled in between the sheets, he felt happy once more.

And everyone else on the farm felt better too. They all fell into a deep sleep.

About two hours later, when Flossie was dreaming that Frisky was running away again, and had come into the house to play the piano, she awoke with a start.

Downstairs, something *was* playing the piano!

CHAPTER VI

A HAY WAGON RIDE

FLOSSIE wakened Nan, with whom she was sleeping.

"Nan, Nan," she said, "Frisky's playing the piano!"

"That's silly," her sister answered. She decided Flossie was having a nightmare. "Go back to sleep," she said.

Flossie insisted she had heard music. But there were no more sounds, so she closed her eyes once more.

When morning came everyone was astir early. A happy day was promised. Frisky was back unharmed, and there was to be a picnic!

"I shan't be able to go on the picnic with you," said the twins' father. "I must go back to Lakeport."

"Oh, Daddy!" the twins chorused.

Mr. Bobbsey promised to come back the

following evening. With a twinkle in his eye he said they should save up some of the fun for him. His children assured him they would.

"I'm going out and see Frisky," Freddie announced, even before his breakfast had been served.

The little boy went to the barn and told the calf how naughty she had been to run away and drag Freddie by the rope, and how he had tried to be like a fireman and save her.

But Frisky did not seem to care a bit about ropes or firemen, but just chewed and chewed some hay, as if there were nothing in this world to do but eat.

"Come on, Freddie," called Dinah, poking her head in the barn door. "You can help me pick berries for breakfast, and I'll look for some radishes for the picnic."

"I don't like radishes," said Freddie, as they reached the vegetable garden. "They burn my tongue."

"Not the little ones from the early crop," said Dinah. "They are nice and sweet. See those little red things peekin' above the ground? They're the ripe ones. We must only pull them."

Freddie was still sure he did not want to eat the radishes, but he bent down to look at them.

He got so close that a disturbed toad hopped right up at his nose.

"Oh!" he cried in surprise. "Dinah, will he bite?"

"Land sakes, no! That poor little toady is more scared than you," and she pointed to the big dock leaf under which the hoptoad was now hiding.

"Let's pick beans," Freddie suggested, liking them better than radishes.

"Not today," laughed Dinah. "Whoever heard of beans on a picnic?"

"That stuff there, then," the boy persisted, pointing to the soft green leaves of early lettuce.

"Well, I dunno. Martha didn't say so, but it sure does look pretty. Yes, I guess we can pick some for salad." And so Dinah showed Freddie how to cut the lettuce heads off and leave the stalks to grow again. Then they went over to the raspberry canes.

As Freddie and Dinah came down the path ten minutes later with a small basket of vegetables and raspberries, they met Uncle Daniel.

"Out early," he laughed.

"Is it?" Freddie asked, meaning early, of course, in his funny little way of getting words mixed up. "When is 'early' over?"

Uncle Daniel laughed and walked on.

"See! See!" called Flossie, running up with

Nan to Freddie and Dinah. "See what we've got!"

In a large white bowl were luscious red strawberries from everbearing plants. Seeing the raspberries in Freddie's basket, she said:

"Mine are bigger."

But Freddie was not going to be outdone by his sister. "My red—radishes are redder," he argued.

Nan and Dinah laughed.

"Maybe our berries are sweeter," said Nan, teasing her little brother.

"Our—our radishes are hotter," said Freddie, and this ended the argument.

After breakfast Martha and Dinah began packing the lunch. Flossie and Freddie stayed in the kitchen to watch what was going on. The two cooks made the children laugh merrily with their funny stories.

"This reminds me," said Martha, "of something that happened when I was a little girl. We had two baskets exactly alike. One time when my brother and I were going to a Sunday school picnic, my brother picked up the wrong basket. When we got to the picnic, we had nothing to eat. In the basket was a blanket my mother was sending to a neighbour's horse!"

Dinah chuckled. "One time when I was just

a young 'un, my mother made a great big custard pie and it sure looked good. She set it on the back porch to cool, and what you think? When it came time for dessert, there was nothin' left of the pie but the crust. Our sassy little hound dog done ate all the middle out of the pie!"

Freddie and Flossie laughed, and begged for more stories.

Meanwhile, Uncle Daniel, Bert, and Harry had gone off to collect the other boys and girls who were going on the picnic. When they returned, Nan was surprised to see a boy named Mark Teron with them. She had heard her twin say few boys around Meadow Brook liked him.

"How'd you happen to bring Mark?" she whispered to Bert.

Her brother said they could not very well get out of it, because Mark was at Tom Mason's house when they got there. Everyone hoped that Mark would not play one of his mean tricks.

Besides Tom and Mark there were Jack Hopkins and August Stout, friends of Harry. Then there were Mildred Manners and Mabel Herold, who were Nan's age. Roy Mason, Tom's small brother, and Bessie Dimple had come as playmates for Freddie and Flossie.

Uncle Daniel explained that they were not going to the picnic in the station wagon, but in the big hay wagon. It was to be pulled by Meadow Brook's two lovely horses, Billy and Betty. Harry helped hitch up the team while the other boys got nice fresh hay and spread it on the bottom of the wagon.

"Say," said Uncle Daniel to his son, "how would you like to take two homing pigeons along? You could send a note back to Martha to say what time you would be home."

"Great!" chorused all the boys, instantly making a run for the pigeon house.

"Wait!" Harry told his friends. "We must be careful not to scare them." He went inside the wire cage alone with a handful of corn. "See —de—coon! See—de—coon!" he called softly, imitating the queer sounds made by the doves cooing.

Harry tossed the corn on the floor. Then, as the two pigeons he wanted came to taste the food, he took them in his arms.

"How do you tie the message on their legs?" asked Freddie Bobbsey, who had come out to see what was going on.

"The right way," Harry answered, "is to fasten a little aluminium capsule around one leg. The message goes inside the capsule."

"Let me get one," said Freddie.

Harry said that unfortunately he did not have

any capsules. He usually just tied the message around the pigeons' legs with a thread. Being good pigeons, they did not peck them off.

Soon everything was ready for the picnic. The children climbed into the big wagon one by one, and nestled down in the sweet-smelling hay. Then Mrs. Bobbsey and Aunt Sarah were helped aboard by Uncle Daniel. Finally he climbed up to the high seat in front. He took the reins in his strong hands, and smiled down at the children, who were eager to start. Then, turning to the horses, he said:

"Giddap, Billy! Giddap, Betty! We're off for the picnic grove!"

CHAPTER VII

FUN ON A PICNIC

IT WAS a beautiful day, and the well-groomed horses stepped along in lively fashion, as if they, too, enjoyed the thought of a picnic. While the picnickers were having their lunch, Billy and Betty would find nice green grass and wild flowers in the grove.

After the picnickers had been riding about twenty minutes, they came to a roadside spring. August Stout called out:

"Let's stop for a drink." August, who was stout by name and size, loved a good drink of water.

The children scrambled out of the hay wagon, and took turns getting a drink. There was a round basin built of stones and quite deep. Into this the clear water trickled from a little cave in the hill above.

"Oh, what a cute little pond!" Flossie exclaimed.

"Are there any fish in it? I don't want to drink a fish."

There was no cup or dipper from which to drink, so Flossie knew she would have to put her mouth right down in the water.

"We'll see if there are any fish," said Nan.

She looked, but there was not a sign of one, so Flossie put her head down. In the end she got her whole face wet and came up sputtering.

Meanwhile, Mark Teron had been standing off to one side, talking to August. "Bert Bobbsey thinks he's better'n the rest of us 'cause he comes from the city," Mark complained. "I don't like him."

"He seems like a regular fellow to me," August answered.

Mark waited until it was Bert's turn to take a drink. Then he stepped up behind him. The next thing Bert knew, his head was pushed down under the water and held there.

He tried to raise it up but couldn't. His nose and mouth were filled with water. He could not breathe. Just when he felt as if he could not stand it another second, the pressure suddenly stopped.

Gasping for breath, Bert bobbed up and looked around. He was just in time to see his cousin Harry land a blow on Mark's chest.

"You mean kid!" Harry cried. "You leave my cousin alone!"

"I didn't hurt the big sissy," Mark answered, trying to punch Harry back.

"Stop your fighting, both of you!" Uncle Daniel ordered. "Get in the wagon! And, Mark, if you can't behave yourself, you'll have to go home!"

Mark hung his head and climbed in. The other boys and girls followed. No one talked for a while. Then Aunt Sarah said, "Let's sing!" and everyone forgot the unpleasant incident.

They sang all kinds of songs until Uncle Daniel left the road and turned into a wood. He drove for a few minutes among the pines, maples, and oak trees which abounded in the section.

"We'll stop here," Uncle Daniel called down, as they reached a particularly thick grove of pine trees. "Whoa! Whoa! Billy! Betty!"

The picnic things were taken from the hay wagon, and the horses were unhitched. The children began scampering about the lovely glade like so many squirrels.

"Let's build a fireplace," Jack Hopkins suggested.

"Sure," said the other boys, and immediately started gathering stones and piling them up.

There was plenty of wood lying about, and when

a fire was built, the raw potatoes that Harry had secretly brought along were roasted, finer than any indoor oven could cook them.

There were so many pretty little nooks to explore in the woods that Mrs. Bobbsey had to warn the children not to wander too far away or they might get lost. She and Aunt Sarah opened the baskets and spread the tablecloth on the pine needles. Then they decorated it and arranged the places. Presently Bert, who had brought them some water, shouted into the woods:

"Dinner served in the dining car!" imitating the call of a waiter on a train.

"Oh, how pretty!" all the girls exclaimed, as they ran back and beheld the "feast in the forest", as Nan put it.

And indeed it was pretty, for at each place lay a long plume of fern leaves with forget-me-nots at the end, and what could be more beautiful than such a decoration?

"Potatoes first!" Harry announced, "because they may get cold." And at this order everybody sat down on the grass and broke the freshly roasted potatoes on the paper plates, and put on the extra butter that had been brought along.

"Simply wonderful!" declared Nan, with the air of one who recognizes good cooking.

Sandwiches and many other good things were

passed. Then came a surprise. Rich hot chocolate, which the children loved. Martha's big jug had kept it piping hot.

"It's fun to camp out," Mabel Herold remarked. "No dishes to wash," she giggled. Mabel always had a lot of dishes to wash at home.

"Think how soldiers get along with just a mess kit," Bert put in.

Suddenly, Flossie exclaimed, "What's that?"

"A snake, a snake!" called several of the children.

Everyone jumped up and ran except Uncle Daniel and Harry and Bert.

"There he is!" shouted Bert, as the snake tried to crawl under a stump.

"Look out! He's dangerous!" Uncle Daniel declared, as the snake coiled itself, then raised up ready to strike.

Harry, armed with a tree branch he had picked up, sprang forward and dealt the snake a heavy blow on the head that laid it flat.

"Get him! Get him!" called Tom Mason, as the wounded snake lay writhing in the grass.

This time Uncle Daniel with a stone, and Bert with a stick, finished off the dangerous reptile.

"He's a big one!" Harry declared, as he stretched the creature out to measure him. "He's five feet long! A black racer!"

When the excitement died down, the picnic was resumed.

"Do I have to eat so much?" Freddie suddenly sighed. He had been told so often not to help himself to more than he could finish. "I—I'm just ready to bust!"

Uncle Daniel took pity on him and said he would eat his small nephew's cake. Hearing this, Flossie passed to her uncle the piece on her plate because she, too, could eat no more.

Nan smiled. She already had had plenty. Very quietly she got up, and when Uncle Daniel was not looking, Nan slipped her portion on to his plate.

The others waited for him to become aware of the pile of cake. When he did, he laughed loudly, and the others did too.

"Goodness!" exclaimed Uncle Daniel, "I'll feel just like Freddie if I eat all this. I guess I'll get Billy and Betty to help me out."

"The idea!" cried Aunt Sarah. "Feeding my good cake to the horses!"

Finally everyone arose from the picnic table.

"Let's have a game of hide-and-seek," Nan suggested.

In a twinkling every boy and girl was hidden behind a tree, and Nan found herself "It". Of course, it took a big tree to hide the children completely, and Nan had no trouble in spying Mildred first. Soon the game was going along merrily, and the boys and girls were out of breath trying to get "home free".

"Where's Flossie?" asked Nan, after they had been playing a while.

"Hiding somewhere," Roy ventured, for it seemed only a minute before that the little girl had been with the others.

"But where is she?" Nan insisted, as call after call brought no answer.

"Over at the maple tree!" Harry thought.

"Down at the spring," Freddie said.

"Looking for flowers," Bessie guessed.

But all these spots were searched, and the little girl was not found.

Meanwhile everybody searched and searched, but still Flossie could not be found.

CHAPTER VIII

FOURTH OF JULY

BY THIS time the older Bobbseys had become very much concerned about Flossie's absence. Surely she could not still be playing a game.

"Maybe she went down to the river," ventured Tom Mason, who had been there to swim several times.

"Oh, my goodness!" cried Mr. Bobbsey, because Flossie could not swim very well.

Tom was already running toward the water. The older boys and girls kept up to him, and got to the river long before the grown-ups and the small children.

"There's Flossie!" cried Nan. "Out in a boat all by herself!"

Sure enough, there sat little Flossie Bobbsey in the rowboat a good distance from shore. She was looking happily into the water and trailing one hand in it.

"We'll have to swim out and get her!" declared Bert. "Can you fellows swim?"

"Sure," they answered, taking off their shirts and moccasins.

Two oars lay on the shore. Quickly Bert handed one of them to Harry and Jack. He and Tom took the other.

"Come on, fellows!" he said.

The four waded in with the oars, then started swimming. By this time the older Bobbseys had run up. They were relieved to see Flossie, but Aunt Sarah called out:

"She's drifting toward the dam!"

Not a great way down the river was an old water-wheel and a dam. Should the boat drift there, Flossie might be dashed over it. It was hard work for the boys to swim, pushing the oars ahead, but they went as fast as they could.

"Easy now!" called Bert finally. "Hi, Flossie! Don't get up!" her brother warned her. Bert was afraid that in her excitement she might fall overboard.

He and Tom climbed carefully into the boat, one from each side, so as not to tip it over. Jack and Harry were not long in following. Quickly Harry started rowing to shore, while Bert put his arm around his little sister and asked why she had gone off alone.

"I wanted to hide awfully good," Flossie said. "When the boat floated around, it was fun."

"But dangerous," her brother told her, explaining about the dam.

"Oh-o-o!" said Flossie with a shiver. "I'll never do it again."

When the little group of boatmen reached the shore, everyone talked at once. The boys received plenty of praise for the rescue.

"You fellows had your swim ahead of time," grinned Uncle Dan. "Better put on your swimming trunks now and let your dungarees dry."

All the children had brought bathing suits, and now got them from the hay wagon, and went to the beach house to change their clothes.

For the next two hours the older children dived and had races and played games along the river bank. The water was too deep for the small children, so they waded in a shallow pool near the beach house, and sailed an old toy boat.

At four o'clock Aunt Sarah called out, "Time to let the pigeons loose!"

No one wanted to miss seeing this, so all the Bobbsey children and their friends dashed out of the water. Aunt Sarah said they must dress first. When everyone was ready, they hurried back to the grove where the hay wagon was.

Harry took a piece of tissue paper and a pencil

from his pocket. Aunt Sarah said to write on it, "Home at five-thirty. Supper at six." •

While no one was looking, Mark Teron had taken the pigeons' cage from the hay wagon. He opened the door. Quick as a wink, one of the pigeons got out and soared into the air.

"Oh!" cried Nan, who happened to turn around at that moment and see what was happening.

She dashed up to Mark and grabbed the second pigeon just as it started to fly away.

"You horrid boy!" she cried, very angry at Mark for trying to spoil the game.

Nan carried the pigeon to Harry, who tied the message around one of its legs with a tiny, but strong cord. Then he called, "All ready!"

Snap! went something that sounded like a shot (but it wasn't), and away flew the pretty bird to take the message home to Martha. The "shot" was only a dry stick that Tom Mason snapped to imitate a gun, as they do at races, but the effect was quite startling and made the others jump.

"What time will the pigeon get home?" Flossie asked.

"In about fifteen minutes," Harry answered.

"Gee, I wish I was a pigeon," Freddie sighed. He liked to ride fast.

When it was time to go home, Uncle Daniel

told Mark to sit at the front with him in the hay wagon, so he could not play any more tricks. Everyone hopped aboard and they started off. The first stop was Mark's house. The thoughtless boy did not even say "thank you", or "I had a good time", or even "good-bye" as he ran off.

"We'll never invite him again," Harry declared.

The other children were dropped off one by one, and at exactly five-thirty the Bobbseys reached Meadow Brook Farm.

"Just like the pigeon's message said," smiled Martha, and Flossie was glad to hear that both pigeons had reached the farm safely.

The twins had had so much fun at the picnic that they were sure it was the best kind of day they could think of. But the next morning Harry had an even more exciting suggestion to offer.

"You know what tomorrow is?" he asked Bert, as the two boys were dressing the next morning.

"Friday, July fourth," Bert answered.

"How much money you got?" said his cousin.

"A dollar. Why?"

"I have a dollar, too," said Harry. "What do you say we go to town on the two bikes here, and buy some fireworks for tomorrow? We'd better get our stuff early, for Stimpson's sold out before noon last year."

"Swell," Bert grinned. "Let's keep it a secret.

But we'll get sparklers for Freddie and Flossie, and Chinese crackers for Nan," he said, as they started for the little country grocery store soon after breakfast.

"I guess I'll buy a few snakes, they look so funny coiling out after they're lighted," said Harry.

But at Stimpson's store the boys had to take just what they could get, as the supply was very limited and several other boys were already there buying.

"Let's have a celebration tomorrow," Tom Mason suggested.

"Got anything in mind?" Harry asked.

"How about a soap-box race?"

This was talked over, but since only a few boys had made soap boxes into scooters, it was decided to have a bicycle race instead. Harry and Tom were elected to map out a course with several obstacles in it.

"We could start on Main Street," said Harry, "and then turn up Knob Hill."

"How about down the lane at the top," suggested Tom, "and across the brook——" Tom stopped to chuckle. "I'll bet a lot of the fellows will fall off there and lose time."

"You're right," grinned Harry. "And let's make the last part of the ride hard. Through the old sand pit, and then back to Main Street. The first fellow to reach Stimpson's wins!"

When he and Bert reached home, they told the girls and Freddie about the plan. "Why don't you do something, too?" Bert added.

Now there was one thing both Freddie and Flossie loved—a parade. So they announced at once that this was what they wanted.

"All right," said Nan. "I'll help you."

"Let's keep it a secret from the big people," Flossie begged.

Bert and Harry started a canvass from house to house, to get all the boys in Meadow Brook who owned bicycles to take part in the celebration.

"Can the little children do something, too?" August Stout asked.

"Yes, they're going to have a parade," Bert answered.

"Be sure to bring your flag for one of them to carry," said his cousin.

"How about using my goat and wagon?" asked Jack, when they reached his house.

"Freddie will be sure to use it," laughed Bert. "I'll tell him about it."

"We'll meet at ten o'clock tomorrow morning in our lane," said Harry.

While the boys were gone, Nan decided that the girls should take part in the celebration too.

She telephoned to Mildred and Mabel, and suggested a play. They loved the idea, and said they would get some more girls to be in it. Later, ten of them came over for a meeting.

Such chatter and giggling! They could not decide on what the play might be, until Aunt Sarah made a suggestion.

"I have something precious packed away in a trunk that you may use, Nan," she said, getting into the spirit of Independence Day. "A real Betsy Ross flag, one with thirteen stars, you know. How about a play around the flag?"

"Oh, yes, Betsy Ross made the first flag, didn't she?" remarked Mildred, trying to remember her history.

"It would be wonderful to use the flag," said Nan.

It was a busy day for everybody, and when Mr. Bobbsey came up on the train from Lakeport that evening, they found he, too, had been busy. He had brought boxes and boxes of fireworks for the boys and girls, and even some for the grown folks.

The Bobbsey children could hardly sleep that night, they were so excited over the celebration.

"Are you awake, Bert?" called Harry, so early the next morning that the sun was hardly up yet.

"Yep," replied his cousin, jumping out of bed

and hastily dressing for the firing of the first salute.

The boys crept through the house very quietly, then ran to the barn for their ammunition. Three giant fireworks were placed in the drive directly in front of the house.

"Be careful!" whispered Bert. "They're full of powder." The next instant there was a thunderous report.

Bang! Bang! Bang!

CHAPTER IX

A BIG BALLOON

"HURRAH!" shouted Freddie Bobbsey from his bedroom window. "It's Fourth of July!"

He dressed quickly and came downstairs. All the others were aroused by the early salutes, and in a short time there were also many boys from other farms. The Bobbsey boys were firing so many kinds of fireworks that Meadow Brook sounded as if it were being attacked!

"Ouch!" yelled Tom Mason, the first one to burn his fingers. "A banger caught me right on the thumb."

But such small accidents were not given much attention, and soon Tom was lighting the little red crackers as merrily as before. Nan joined them, and had an exciting time too!

Freddie and Flossie were having great fun throwing their little sparklers at the stone terrace that surrounded the well.

The Bobbsey children were having such fun that they could hardly be induced to come into breakfast, but when the visiting boys ran off across the fields to their homes, the twins finally did stop long enough to eat.

"It's time to get ready!" whispered Nan to Bert, as the hands of the clock reached ten.

She ran off to the old carriage house, and found several small boys and girls waiting and eager to arrange their costumes. The older girls were in white, and were to wear a ribbon decoration.

"Just put the ribbon over your right shoulder and tie it loosely under your left arm," ordered Captain Nan, and the girls obeyed as quickly as if they had been cadets.

The broad red, white, and blue ribbons looked very pretty over the girls' white dresses, and indeed the "cadets" looked as if they might outdo the boys, who had put red, white, and blue bunting on their bicycles.

"Where's Nettie?" asked Nan suddenly, missing the little girl who was to be one of Flossie's attendants. Flossie herself was to be the Goddess of Liberty.

"Nettie wouldn't come because she had no white dress," Mildred answered.

"Oh, what a shame! She'll be so disappointed! Besides, we need her," said Nan. "Just wait."

Before the others could guess what she was going to do, Nan ran off to the house, got one of Flossie's white dresses, rolled it up neatly, and was over the fields at Nettie's house in a few minutes. When Nan came back she brought Nettie with her, looking very sweet and happy in the borrowed dress.

Next Flossie had to be dressed. She was to wear a light blue dress with gold stars on it, and on her pretty yellow curls was placed a real Liberty crown. She carried the cleanest, brightest flag of all, and what a pretty picture she made!

"Oh, isn't she sweet!" all the girls exclaimed in admiration.

"There go the drums!" Nan declared. "Come on!"

The girls and boys met at the end of the driveway near the barn, where two boys who did not own bicycles were to beat the drums and lead the parade.

"Hurrah! Hurrah!" shouted the boys from their bicycles.

"Oh, you girls look great!" exclaimed Harry.

Some of the small boys had on red, white, and blue hats. Several were dressed like soldiers and sailors, and members of the Marine and Air Corps. Two were Revolutionary soldiers and were tooting fifes they had borrowed.

"And Freddie!" exclaimed Bert. "Isn't he a grand Uncle Sam!"

Freddie was dressed in the striped suit Uncle Sam always wears, and on his head was a tall white hat. He was to ride in Jack Hopkins' goat wagon.

"Fall in!" called Nan, and at the word all the boys and the girls fell in line for the march.

Flossie and her attendants were to be the very first in line after the drummers. Then came Freddie as Uncle Sam in the goat wagon.

"Left, right, left, right! Forward march!" called Nan, and the procession started up the driveway toward the house.

"Goodness gracious sakes alive! Do come see the children! That sure is a nice parade!" called Dinah, running outside to view the procession.

"Oh, isn't it just beautiful!" Martha echoed, close on Dinah's heels.

"My!" exclaimed Mrs. Bobbsey. "How did they ever get fixed up so cleverly?" The whole thing had been kept a secret from the twins' parents.

"And look at Flossie and Freddie!" exclaimed their father proudly. "We must get the camera!"

Freddie's chariot was now in line with the

grown-up audience, and he raised his tall hat to them like a real Uncle Sam.

By this time Mr. Bobbsey had returned with the camera.

"Halt!" called Harry, and the procession stood still.

"Look this way. There now, all ready," said Mr. Bobbsey, and snap went the camera on a very pretty picture.

"Forward march!" called Nan again, and amid drumming and tooting the procession started off to parade through the village of Meadow Brook.

Since it was a long walk, Uncle Daniel got out the station wagon, and Mr. Bobbsey the truck, and the children were driven to the edge of the town. They hopped out and got in line again.

Never before had such a parade been seen in the little country town, and all along the main street cheer after cheer greeted the marchers. By eleven o'clock the procession had made the complete circuit of the little town, and the onlookers walked up to the schoolhouse to see the girls' play.

The boys were itching to start their race, but they sat and listened politely, and clapped loudly when the show was over. Nan was lovely as Betsy Ross, and spoke her lines well.

Mildred was George Washington coming to ask

Betsy to make the first flag. Mabel, Marie, and Anna were the needlewomen who helped her sew the stripes together and put on the stars.

Dinah and Martha were sitting in the back of the little auditorium. When Nan said, "General Washington, I present this flag to you. May honour and glory come to our country!" tears rolled down Martha's cheeks.

"Ain't that touching?" she whispered.

"Indeed it is," Dinah replied, sniffing a bit herself. "Glory be to the U.S.A.!"

As soon as the audience filed out, the boys ran for their bicycles and the race started. Everyone watched to see who would win.

What a ride! First one boy ahead, then another! At the brook off went Bert, then Jack. By the time they got started again, the others were pedalling across the field toward the sand pit.

Here everyone got into trouble. The sand slowed down their speed to a point where the boys found it impossible to keep their balance. Some laughed, some became angry.

Finally, Harry had an idea. He walked back to the edge of the pit, then rode around near the rim of it where the sand was drier and firmer. Reaching the far side, he raced for the main street of Meadow Brook.

"Here comes Harry! He's first!" cried Freddie.

The other boys had given up, and came straggling in. They all agreed that Harry deserved to win for figuring out how to get across the sand pit.

Aunt Sarah invited all the children to come back to the Bobbsey farm. The small twins and their friends, as well as the older ones, were glad to ride back, as they had had an exciting morning.

They found a feast ready for them. Aunt Sarah, Dinah, and Martha had set out all kinds of good things to eat on a long table under the trees. There were two kinds of ice-cream, besides cookies and cake. Ice-cold lemonade was passed. Certainly the tired young paraders, actresses, and cyclists had delicious refreshment!

"My goat almost ran away once when Bert let go of him!" announced Freddie, a cookie in each hand. "But I held on real tight."

"Did you see me fall down?" giggled Mildred. "I was watching Uncle Sam and stepped right in a hole."

Harry told the group an old Revolutionary War cannon was going to be shot off at three o'clock. He would like to go watch it and take the other boys.

"They're foolish to put powder in that cracked gun," remarked Uncle Daniel. "Take care that you all keep at a safe distance."

It was not long until three o'clock, and the boys hurried off to see the old cannon. Peter Burns, who had found the Bobbseys' calf, Frisky, was to fire it.

A crowd of people had gathered on the bank of the pond, where the cannon stood. The farmer was busy stuffing powder in the old gun.

"Let's go up on that big tree limb," suggested Bert. "We can see everything and still be out of the range of fire."

So the boys climbed up in the low willow that leaned over the pond bank.

"They're almost ready," Harry said, seeing the crowd scatter.

"Look out!" yelled Peter Burns, getting hold of the long string that would fire the gun.

He gave it a tug, then another. Everybody held his breath, expecting to hear an awful bang, but the cannon did not go off.

Very cautiously Peter stepped nearer, to see what might be the matter. The next instant, with a terrific report, the whole cannon flew up in the air!

Peter fell back! His hat seemed to go up with the gun!

"Oh, he's killed!" yelled several people.

By this time the crowd had surrounded the old man, who lay very still and white.

"He's only unconscious from the shock," spoke up Jack Hopkins' father, who was a doctor. "He'll be all right."

Presently the old man opened his eyes and looked around. Then he sat up and asked in a shaky voice:

"Did it go off?"

"It sure did," the doctor smiled. "And you went with it. How do you feel?"

"Oh, I'll be all right when my head clears a bit."

The crowd scattered, and the boys went back to Meadow Brook Farm. They had hardly finished telling about the exciting incident, when Freddie called out:

"Look at the balloon!"

"It's going to land in our orchard," said Harry, as everyone looked up toward the sky.

They hurried to the orchard. The children never had seen such a big balloon. Uncle Daniel said he had not seen an "old-timer" like this one for many, many years.

"Well, where'd it come from?" Freddie asked excitedly.

"Probably from the Farmers' Picnic," his uncle replied. "They're having an old-fashioned aviation display there today and I suppose the balloon is part of it."

When the balloon came lower, the children gasped in astonishment.

"Look! There's a man hanging to it!" Nan cried out. And the next moment a parachute shot out from the balloon with a man dangling from it.

"Oh, he'll fall!" cried Freddie. "Let's catch him in something!"

CHAPTER X

THE LITTLE GARDENERS

UNCLE DANIEL took hold of Freddie's hand.

"I'm sure the balloon man will be all right," he said. "He's used to doing this. You see, that parachute keeps him from coming down too quickly."

"How does it?" Freddie asked.

"The air gets under the 'chute and holds it up. The man's weight then brings it down gently."

"Here he comes! Here he comes!" the boys called, as the big parachute, with the man dangling from it, floated down—down beside a harvest-apple tree!

"Hallo there!" he called, quickly picking himself up from the ground and gathering up the folds of the parachute.

"Hallo yourself!" answered Harry. "Did you have a nice ride?" he added, grinning.

"First class," replied the man.

The children were delighted to talk to a person who had been up in the balloon, and asked him a hundred questions.

Just then the balloon itself, which had been tossing about, getting flatter and flatter, came down in the field at the far end of the orchard.

"Well, there!" exclaimed the stunt man. "That's good luck. Now, whoever of you boys gets that balloon first will get ten dollars. That's what the Farmers' Picnic pays anyone for bringing it back!"

With a dash every boy started for the spot where the balloon had landed. Ned Prentice, Nettie's brother, was one of the best runners, and he cut across the orchard to get a clear way out of the crowd.

"Get it, Bert!" called Freddie.

"Keep it up, Harry!" yelled someone else.

"You'll reach it first, Tom!" came another voice.

"They've got it," cried the excited girls a few minutes later.

"It's Harry!"

"No, it's Bert!"

"'Tisn't either—it's my brother Ned!" called Nettie, jumping up and down for joy.

"Three cheers for Ned!" called Uncle Daniel.

"Hurrah! Hurrah!" shouted all the boys good-naturedly, for Ned was a favourite with everybody.

"Suppose we drive to the Farmers' Picnic," Uncle Daniel suggested. "Then Ned can turn in the balloon, and get his ten dollars. And we'll take you along," he told the balloon man.

Uncle Daniel brought around the big station wagon, and all the boys piled in with the stunt man.

Ned was very happy as he was awarded the money half an hour later. When they reached his house, the boy proudly put the ten-dollar bill in his mother's hand.

"Be sure to come up to our fireworks tonight," Harry called, as they drove away, and Ned promptly accepted the invitation.

"It has certainly been a great Fourth of July!" Uncle Daniel exclaimed, when the children fired off their Roman candles and skyrockets.

The little children had beautiful pinwheels and sparklers that they set off on the lawn. Mr. Bobbsey lighted a set piece nailed to a tree. In a moment it began to hiss, then what a beautiful sight!

"It's Niagara Falls!" cried Nan.

This concluded the evening's entertainment, and the children marched off happily to bed.

For a few days after the Fourth it rained, as it always seems to do. Some people say that the noise from all the exploding fireworks shakes up the clouds and makes it rain. This is hard to believe, but just the same, it does seem to rain after the Fourth.

"Suppose you play in the old carriage house," Aunt Sarah told the children the second day, when she could not stand the noise in the house any longer, "but don't keep running in and out and getting wet."

The children promised to obey, and hurried out to the old carriage house which, many years ago, in the horse-and-buggy days, had housed the wagons and carts that were used before motor cars came into use. Now nothing was left but the big hay wagon in which the Bobbseys had ridden to the picnic.

Freddie climbed in the wagon and made believe it was a fire engine. Bert attached a bell on the side for him, and when he pulled a rope, the bell would clang like one on a hook-and-ladder fire engine. Nan and Flossie hopped up on to the back with all the dolls Flossie had brought along, and made believe they were driving to New York to do some shopping.

"Freddie, you be the driver," coaxed Flossie, "because we have to have someone drive us."

"But who will put out all the fires?" argued the little fellow, "'cause they're really truly true."

"I know," Nan suggested. "We will pretend this is a big high coach, like the ones you see in some of the old-fashioned pictures. I'll be away up high on the front, driving four big black horses."

"And somebody always blows a horn," said Freddie. "I'll blow the horn 'cause I got that big fire out now."

Nan got a toy horn from the house. Then Freddie perched himself on the high seat with his sisters and blew the horn until Nan told them they had reached New York and were going to stop for dinner.

They were having such a gay time that before they knew it the morning had passed. It cleared up in the afternoon and John, the farm hand, asked the children if they wanted to help him do some transplanting.

"Oh, we'd love to," Nan answered.

The ground was just right for transplanting, after the rain, and the tender little lettuce plants were as easy to take up as they were to put down again.

"Nan," said John, "how would you like to have a garden all your own? You can have that patch over there. I'll give you a couple of dozen plants, and we will see what kind of a farmer you are."

"Oh, thank you, John," Nan answered. "I'll do just as I've seen you doing," and she began to move the little plants from one bed to the other.

"Be careful not to shake the dirt off the roots," said John, "and be sure to put only one plant in each place. Put them as far apart as the length of this little stick, and when you put them in the ground, press the earth firmly around the roots."

"I want to be a planter, too," called Flossie, running up the path to John.

"All right," John answered. "Suppose you help your sister."

Flossie was delighted to help Nan, and the two girls made a very nice garden indeed.

Besides the lettuce, there was a row of cabbage and one of broccoli. John asked if the girls wanted to plant some seeds for late carrots and beets and turnips, and took several tiny packages from a pocket of his overalls.

"Oh, yes," Nan and Flossie said together.

First, John picked up a drill and made a furrow in the soft ground.

"If it rains again that will be a good play river," said Flossie, who often played river at home with Freddie after a rain.

"Now, you see this seed is very fine," continued John, "so when you plant it, be very careful not to let too many fall in one spot."

Flossie took a package of carrot seeds, and dropped a little shower of them in the furrow.

"They're all gone!" she told John presently. "May I have some more?"

John shook his head. "That will make more carrots than you could eat all winter!" he said. "Now we'll cover them up. See, I just cover the seeds very lightly like your mother covers you when you're asleep in the summer-time."

"Do you cover them more in the winter-time, the way my mummy does me?" Flossie asked.

John laughed. He said he had never planted seeds in the winter-time. But he supposed that would be the thing to do.

"The seeds from the trees and bushes are covered with a thick blanket of snow, aren't they?" he chuckled.

"That's funny," said Flossie, wrinkling her nose because she was puzzled. "Snow's awful cold, but it keeps seeds warm!"

She and Nan helped with the rest of the planting, then asked how soon the seeds would start growing.

"Right away," John answered. "And in about a week, you'll see 'em peeping above the ground."

"I'll come up and tend my garden every morning," Nan declared.

"You'll have to keep it clear of weeds, and if a

dry spell should come, you must water it each day," said John.

Nan kept her word. But a few mornings later, something happened which took her mind off the garden completely for that day. As she was dressing, Nan began rummaging through the bureau drawer where she kept handkerchiefs, scarfs, and jewellery. A minute later she raced to her mother's bedroom, tears in her eyes.

"Oh, Mother," she sobbed, "my lovely pearl necklace—it's gone!"

CHAPTER XI

A RUNAWAY

"YOUR necklace is gone?" Mrs. Bobbsey repeated. "You mean the one Aunt Emily and Uncle William gave you last Christmas?"

"Yes," Nan answered. "I—I guess I lost it."

"That's a shame, but maybe we'll find it. When did you last have it on?"

Nan thought hard. She had worn the necklace at various times. Now she knew she had been foolish to have it on while playing.

"Yesterday I put it on to show Mabel when she came over," Nan answered. "I remember now, I forgot to take it off."

"Where did you go?" her mother asked.

"Oh, so many places. I was down in the garden, and up the lane, and at the well, and out in the barn, and over in the apple orchard, and feeding the chickens, and over in the hayfield—lots of places."

"Then it will be like looking for a needle in a haystack," declared Mrs. Bobbsey, "but we'll all hunt."

The news soon spread that the necklace was lost, and everybody at Meadow Brook Farm set to work searching for it. Bert and Harry chose the barn loft and pitched hay left and right in their search. Flossie and Freddie looked among the flowers and in the vegetable gardens. Mrs. Bobbsey and Aunt Sarah investigated the house thoroughly, even looking under sofa cushions.

A halt was called at lunch-time. No one had had any luck, so the hunt was continued all afternoon. But by five o'clock there was still no success.

"I suppose I'll never see my darling necklace again," sighed Nan.

"Oh, I guess it'll turn up sometime," said Bert hopefully.

Nan went to bed at the usual time, but she was not able to sleep well. She kept waking up, still worried about the missing pearl beads.

"Goodness, I must be dreaming," she told herself one of the times. "No, I'm awake. What's going on?"

From somewhere came little musical sounds. Nan listened attentively.

"It must be the piano," she decided. "But who's playing, and so funny, too?"

The notes came in little runs, then a louder, discordant thump. Suddenly Nan was reminded of the time Flossie had said she heard music in the middle of the night. She got up and went to the top of the stairs. It was all dark below.

A few more notes!

Nan opened her mother's door and told her a ghost must be playing the piano. Mrs. Bobbsey knocked on Uncle Daniel's door. He switched on the lights and went below. The others followed. Nobody was at the piano nor anywhere else in the room.

Uncle Daniel went from room to room, but there was no one around.

"And no ghost," he laughed. "In fact, nothing at all except a piece of cake that someone left on the piano keys."

"And cake can't play," laughed Nan.

For the second time the mystery remained unsolved.

"I wonder who'll hear the music next," said Nan.

Uncle Daniel said he hoped he would, as he wanted to end the whole affair. At breakfast everyone else was told about the musical ghost, and Flossie said proudly:

"I heard him first. And he must be a nice ghost; 'cause he didn't hurt us."

"Say," said Bert, "we ought to set a trap for him."

But no one could figure out the right kind of trap, because they had no idea what size the ghost was.

Harry changed the subject by saying:

"Tom Mason's going to show off his colt this afternoon and we can all take turns riding him."

"That would be swell," said Bert enthusiastically. "But colts are pretty skittish, aren't they?"

Harry said Tom's colt was partly broken. "Anyway, we won't have far to fall, for he's not very tall," Harry laughed.

The boys went off to Tom's house after lunch. Jack Hopkins was already there.

"Where's the colt?" asked Bert.

Tom said Sable was in the barn. "He's so swift, my dad thinks he may be a racehorse some day. Come on, we'll bring him out."

Tom led the way to the stable. He untied Sable, led him outside, and asked Harry if he wanted to be the first to ride the colt.

Harry got on. The little animal made no objection.

"Aren't you going to use a saddle?" said Bert.

Harry explained that it was better for an unbroken colt to get used to a rider before putting a saddle on him. Later they would break him to the saddle.

Now the boy sat up very straight, holding the rope reins which were attached to the bit in Sable's mouth. Snapping a small whip at the colt's side, Harry called:

"Giddap!"

But instead of going forward the little horse tried to sit down!

"Whoa! Whoa!" shouted the boys.

Harry clung to Sable's neck and held on in spite of the colt's back being like a toboggan slide.

"Get up, get up there!" urged Tom, but the contrary colt still continued to sit still.

"Look out! Hold on, Harry!" yelled the boys all at once, for at that instant Sable bolted off like a deer.

"He's running away!" called Bert.

This was plain to be seen, for Harry could turn him neither this way nor that, but had all he could do to stick on the frightened animal's back.

"If Sable throws him, Harry will surely be hurt!" Bert exclaimed, and the boys ran as fast as they could across the field after the runaway.

"Whoa! Whoa! Whoa!" they called to the horse.

This did not make the slightest difference to Sable, who kept on going as if he were in a real race. Suddenly he turned and dashed straight up a hill toward a neighbour's cornfield.

"Oh, gosh!" cried Tom. "Old Mr. Trimble gets sore if you go on his property. He might even have Harry arrested if he breaks the corn."

Of course it was impossible for the excited horse to go through a field of corn and not do any damage.

Harry thought fast.

"If I could only get Sable to that fence over there, he'd have to stop," the boy decided, and gave the left rein a jerk in that direction.

His friends, running at top speed, were fearful that the colt would throw Harry against the fence and injure him. But they did not reckon on Harry's presence of mind. As he reached the fence, the colt was forced to stop, and Harry slid from his back, still holding the reins tightly.

Sable had gone down on his forelegs, ending the runaway's sport.

The other boys rushed up. Tom grinned and said they had better get out of the cornfield. Mr. Trimble's dogs were barking loudly, and would soon reach the spot.

As they quickly led the colt back to the Masons' farm, Bert asked Harry if he was sure he was not hurt, because his cousin was limping badly.

"I feel as if I dropped from an aeroplane on to a pile of rocks," Harry answered. "Gee, Sable sure can go fast. He'll make a racehorse all right."

When they reached the barn and told Mr. Mason, he was relieved that Harry had not been hurt, and decided that the other boys had better not try to ride the skittish colt.

Bert and Tom were disappointed, but found other things to do. This was not the last of the incident, however, for that evening old Mr. Trimble came over to the Bobbsey farm.

Scowling, he stamped on to the front porch and peered right and left, as if trying to find something. Then, when Uncle Daniel went out to meet his neighbour, Mr. Trimble said angrily:

"Where is that scallawag son of yours?"

CHAPTER XII

A NARROW ESCAPE

"MY SON is not a scallawag," Uncle Daniel declared.

"He's going to pay for the damage to my corn-field, and a good fat sum, too!" cried Mr. Trimble.

Knowing how excitable his neighbour was, Uncle Daniel tried to calm him. "I'll see what can be done," he said. "I'm sorry Harry damaged your corn, but he didn't mean to and he's not a scallawag."

"People got no business lettin' animals get on other folks' property," Mr. Trimble grunted.

"Let's be reasonable and not quarrel over an accident," said Harry's father. "If any corn is knocked over, I'll fix it up; if it's broken down, we will pay for the loss. But my son did not do it purposely, and it was worse for him than you think. He's all black and blue from the run-away."

At this the cross neighbour quieted down and said, well, he would see about it. Mr. Trimble was one of those queer people who find it hard to see the difference between an accident and boys' mischief. Perhaps this was because he had no sons of his own and had forgotten what it is like to be young.

Harry limped in and apologized. Then Uncle Daniel and Bert went to the cornfield with Mr. Trimble. They looked carefully at each hill, and with a spade and hoe were able to put back into place the few stalks that had been knocked down in Sable's flight.

"There, now," said Uncle Daniel, "I guess that corn is as good as ever. But if any of it dies, let me know."

So that ended the adventure of the runaway, except for a very lame boy, Harry Bobbsey, who had to limp around stiffly for a day or two. As soon as he felt all right, he suggested to Bert that they and some of the other fellows go fishing the next day.

"Swell," said Bert.

That night he and Harry stayed out late to get worms for bait. They found a lot of night-walkers crawling near the barn.

Bert had a new rod his father had brought from Lakeport, and the other boys had nets as well, like most country boys who live near streams and are fond of fishing.

"Let's go over to the cove," Harry said, when they started off. "There are usually a lot of good fish over there."

So the cove was chosen as the best spot to try their luck, and soon the Bobbsey boys and their friends were sitting around the edge of the deep, clear stream, waiting for a bite.

Bert was the first one to jerk his line, and he brought it up with such force that the chub on his hook slapped Harry right in the face!

"Hey!" cried his cousin, as he dodged the flapping fish. "He's a good one, but I don't want to kiss him!"

The boys laughed. Bert admitted he was a green fisherman. The fish was really a very nice plump chub and weighed more than a pound. It floundered around in the basket and flapped its tail wildly trying to get away from them.

"I've got one!" called Tom, pulling in his line and bringing up a sleek little sunfish. Now sunnies are not considered as good eating as chubs, because they have too many bones, so Tom's catch did not come up to Bert's. But it was put in the basket just the same.

"I'm going out on that tree limb over the water," Stout announced.

"It looks pretty rotten," Tom remarked. "It might break."

"Oh, I'll be all right," August answered, lying down flat on the narrow limb and dropping his line.

For a time all the boys waited for a bite. No one spoke, for it is thought fish are very sensitive to sound and go in another direction if they hear a voice.

They all became so quiet that the little wood-peckers on the trees went on pecking at the tree bark as if no human being was in sight.

Suddenly there was a great crack and a big splash!

"August!" yelled all the boys at once, for the rotten limb had crashed into the water, taking August with it.

They waited for his head to appear above water. When several seconds went by and they did not see him, they became frightened.

"Quick!" said Bert. "He must be under the limb! We must save him!"

In an instant all the boys were in the water, trying to get under the fallen limb. Bert was the first one to spy August. A spiked branch had caught his sweater.

By this time Harry had realized what the trouble was. Together he and Bert pulled August's sweater free, and brought the boy to the surface of the pool. He was unconscious. Quickly they towed him to shore and hauled him on to the bank. August must have artificial respiration at once!

They laid him face down on the grass, and Harry knelt astride him, pressing the palms of his hands against August's back in rhythmical motion. Then Bert did it for a while, just as he had learned in the first-aid class at Lakeport.

They worked over him for some time before he opened his eyes.

"Oh!" he murmured at last, "I'm so sick!"

"I guess you are, August," said Bert, "but you'll be all right soon. You had a narrow escape."

"Gee, thanks a lot," the stout boy said, when he was able to speak. "I'm sorry. I'm afraid I scared all the fish away."

The other boys, relieved that August was all right, grinned at his remark, and agreed with him. The fishing party broke up. As soon as August felt like walking, they started for home.

"You can have my fish, August," said Bert generously.

"And mine, too," Tom added.

August did not feel he was entitled to their gift, but they insisted that he accept the fish.

"I'll never go out on a rotten limb again," declared August. "Not for all the fish in Meadow Brook!"

The boys joked about the accident, but actually it had sobered every one of them, for their stout friend might have been drowned.

The Bobbseys were surprised to see Bert and Harry coming home so soon, and were glad to hear that August was all right.

"Since you're back so early," said Aunt Sarah, "maybe you can lend Peter Burns a hand."

"How?" asked Harry.

His mother said that old Peter Burns had been ill ever since the cannon had exploded on the Fourth of July.

"I guess the shock was too much for him. He has not been able to do any work since. He has a nice crop of peas that he expected to sell. Now there's no one to pick them but Mrs. Burns."

Aunt Sarah added that the day before, Mrs. Burns had hired some boys to pick the peas, but they had pulled up so many plants that she had to stop them.

"We'll go right over," said Harry. "How about it, Bert?"

"Sure," said Bert, "and how about phoning Tom and Jack to help?"

Aunt Sarah thought this was a good idea, so

Harry went to the telephone and called his friends. "Meet you there," he said, hanging up.

Mrs. Burns was delighted to see the boys, who promised to pick the peas very carefully and not ruin the plants.

She said she would go along to the pea patch. They climbed into a truck filled with bushel baskets, and Mrs. Burns drove down the lane. When they reached the field where the peas were growing, the boys hopped out. Each took a basket.

"I'll go down this row and you take that," suggested Bert to Harry. "Then we can talk to each other without hollering."

"All right," Harry replied, snapping the peas off the plants and dropping them into his basket.

"Let's have a race," called Tom. "See who gets a basket full first."

"But no skipping for big ones," put in Jack. "You have to pick every one that's filled out."

The boys worked two rows at a time. They were so interested in the race that scarcely a word was spoken. The peas were plentiful, so that the baskets were filling up quickly. Mrs. Burns herself was picking; in fact, she had been in the field off and on since dawn.

"You are fine pickers," she told the boys, seeing

how quickly they worked. "I pay twenty-five cents a basket, you know."

"I guess we can earn plenty of money at this rate," laughed Tom, whose basket was almost full.

"I'm done," called Jack from his row. Just then he slipped. "Oh! There goes my basket!"

Sure enough the big basket had been upset in Jack's fall, and most of the peas were scattered on the ground.

"Ha! Ha!" laughed Bert. "I'm first. My basket's full."

"I'm next!" called Tom, picking his basket up in his arms. "I'll carry this to the truck."

"Well, I'll be last, I guess," grinned Jack, trying hard to pick up the scattered peas.

"There's mine!" called Harry, and now all the boys carried their baskets to the truck at the end of the field.

"At this rate it won't take long to fill all the baskets," Mrs. Burns praised them. "Peter will be tickled pink to have them ready, for tomorrow is market day."

The boys worked right on until lunch-time. Each one filled four baskets.

"Well, I declare!" said Mrs. Burns. "Isn't that splendid! But I can't pay you until I get back from market."

"We just did it for fun," Harry spoke up. "We don't want any pay."

"Indeed you must have a dollar apiece, twenty-five cents a basket," she insisted. "See what a good load you have picked!"

"No, really, Mrs. Burns, Mother wouldn't like me to take the money," Bert declared. "We are glad to have helped you, and it was fun."

Poor Mrs. Burns was so grateful that she had to wipe her eyes with her gingham apron.

"Well," she said finally, "there are some folks in this world who talk about charity, but who don't often do anything about it. The crop would have been spoiled tomorrow. You've saved us a great loss."

That afternoon the boys started to the river for a swim. While crossing the Hopkins' field, Jack suddenly yelled:

"Our bull's loose! Run!"

They started racing, but Bert, who was in the rear, did not get far. He stepped in a furrow, turned his ankle, and fell. The others did not notice it.

On galloped the bull! As Bert picked himself up, the big animal was not far from him. He never could outrace him!

"What'll I do?" thought poor Bert. "What would—what would a bullfighter do?"

Bert had seen pictures of bullfighters. Suddenly he knew what to do. As the bull lunged towards him, Bert jumped aside, then raced for the fence in the opposite direction to which the bull was facing.

By the time the big animal got his bearings and discovered where the boy was heading, he was too late to catch him. Bert got safely over the fence!

"That was a close call!" said Harry, as Bert joined the other boys.

"I don't want a repeat of it," laughed Bert. "And whew, I'm hot! Let's get in the river!"

In the meantime, Jack had run home through another field and warned his father about the bull.

"Is he on the rampage again?" exclaimed Mr. Hopkins. "I don't see how he got loose. He's got the strength of a giant!"

It took three men, working cautiously for twenty minutes, to capture the giant. The boys watched from a safe distance.

"I guess my dad will have to sell the bull," said Jack, as they went towards the river. "No matter what we do, he gets loose, and he's awful ugly."

"That's a shame," said Harry. "Well, I'm first in the water."

The boys swam around for half an hour, then climbed up on the bank to rest and talk.

"Say, fellows," said Tom, a little later, "what do you say we stage a circus?"

CHAPTER XIII

PLANNING A CIRCUS

"A CIRCUS sounds great," said Bert and the other boys. "But what could we have for a show?"

"Animals. We have plenty of 'em around here," said Tom.

"Not circus animals," said Harry, "unless you mean Sable."

At this the boys laughed, remembering the runaway.

"Listen, fellows," spoke up Tom, "I rode him yesterday, and he went all right. I could be a cowboy and ride him."

"We could have Frisky as the Sacred Calf," Bert grinned.

"And Snoop as the Wildcat," said Harry, laughing at the thought.

"And August's trained goat," Jack added.

"Then a cage of pigeons," suggested Harry.

"Let's get them all in training," said Tom, jumping up suddenly, eager to begin carrying out their plan.

"I tell you!" Harry said. "We can each train our own animals and then bring them together."

"When will we have the circus?" Jack asked.

"Next week," Tom thought, and a date was decided upon.

During the interval the boys were so busy training their pets that they had little time for other sports. Freddie and the girls wanted to be in the circus too, but they could think of nothing to offer. Nan suggested they go into the woods and maybe they could find something. So off the three trotted. When they returned an hour later, their mother asked if they had had any luck.

"No, but we had a lot of fun," Nan answered. "Once, when Flossie and Freddie were sitting on an old stump, two rabbits ran right across the road in front of them. Freddie thought he'd get them for the circus and ran as fast as he could, but he couldn't go as fast as a rabbit."

"And the squirrels," Flossie spoke up. "I think the squirrels are the prettiest things that live in the woods. They have such bushy tails, Mummy, and they sit up so cute. But we couldn't catch one."

"Oh, I think the rabbits are the nicest," said

Freddie, "'cause they are bunnies, and bunnies bring Easter eggs!" He laughed. "I'm going outside and maybe I *can* find one right on the farm for the circus. I can play make-him-come-out-of-a-hat like a 'gician." Freddie meant magician, of course.

But though he waited, no rabbit appeared, and finally Freddie gave up and started for the barn. Suddenly he saw a mouse run out from under a pile of brushwood.

"Maybe there are some more mice under there," thought Freddie excitedly, pulling away the brushwood. The next moment he yelled, "Come here, everybody! Come quick! Look what I found for the circus!"

Nan and Flossie hurried outside to where their little brother pointed to a nest.

"Field mice!" exclaimed Nan. "Oh, aren't they cute! Let's catch them. Call Bert and Harry."

While Flossie ran to tell the boys, Nan watched the tiny mice so that they would not get away.

"We'll put them in a cage and have them in our circus," said Harry, coming up.

"But they're my mice," cried Freddie, "and I won't let anybody have them!"

"We're only going to help you take care of them," said Bert. "Oh, there's the mother! Let's catch her!"

The mother mouse was not so easy to catch, however, and the boys had a good chase after her. At last she ran into a tin can that had been sunk in the ground for practising sinking golf balls. Harry captured the frightened little creature.

"I'll get a cage," he said. "We can put all the mice in it."

When they were in their new home, Bert went to the kitchen for some cheese.

"What! Feed mice!" exclaimed Dinah. "Sakes alive, child, don't you go bringin' mice in the house to eat all our cake and pie."

"We'll keep them away from the house," Bert promised Dinah. "We're going to have a circus, you know, and these will be our trained mice."

Freddie, of course, was delighted with his find, and wanted to look for more things for the circus.

"I'll tell you!" said Bert. "We might catch butterflies and have them under a big glass on the same table with all the small animals."

"That would be good," Harry agreed. "We could catch some big brown ones and some little fancy ones. Then after dark we could get some big moths on the screen door, after the lights are turned on."

The girls, too, started catching butterflies. Nan was able to net four or five yellow ones in the flower garden near the porch, and Flossie got two of the small brown variety in the nasturtium bed. Harry and Bert searched in the thick syringa bushes where nests were often found.

"Oh, look at this one!" called Freddie, coming up with a great green butterfly. "Is it a bird?" he asked. "See how big it is!"

It really was very large, and had such beautiful wings it might easily be mistaken for some strange bird.

"We'll try to keep them alive," said Harry, and went off to rig up a net enclosure for them.

"Say!" exclaimed Bert, after the butterflies had been taken care of, "couldn't we have an aquarium with water snakes and turtles and frogs?"

"Fine!" declared Harry. "I have a big glass tank I used to have goldfish in. We'll get the other fellows to help catch some water snakes, and fish, and turtles, and frogs, and—and anything else that lives in water!"

Then what a time they had hunting for reptiles! It seemed as if each farm had a different species. August Stout brought three turtles and Jack Hopkins caught two snakes under a stone near their barn. Tom Mason supplied four lovely goldfish, and Ned Prentice brought three bright green frogs.

"I can catch hoptoads," declared Freddie, and

sure enough the little fellow did catch two big ones and a baby toad in his hat. He took them to the older boys, who had their collection in a covered box in the barn.

"We can't put the snakes in with the others or they'll eat them up," said Jack. "I'll get a big glass jar for the snakes."

The circus plans were going along very well. The children could hardly wait for the big day.

"Shall we charge admission to the show?" Bert asked.

"Sure—ten cents each," said Harry, "and give the money to the Meadow Brook Fresh Air Camp over on the mountain."

This was considered a good plan, and now it was only a few days more until Wednesday—the day of the circus!

News about the show spread from one end of Meadow Brook village to the other. Every boy and girl in the neighbourhood planned to see the sights. Even some grown-ups had made up their minds to go too, if only to swell the fresh air fund.

Mrs. Bobbsey, Aunt Sarah, Dinah, and Martha had bought tickets for reserved seats. These cost twenty-five cents each. Mildred Manners was going to bring her mother and her big sister, and Mabel Herold expected to have her mother with her also.

Mr. Bobbsey was coming up from Lakeport purposely to see the circus, and Uncle Daniel had helped the boys put up the seats and fix things generally.

A big tent had been borrowed from the Herolds. It was erected in the open field between the Bobbsey and the Mason farms, alongside a track where Tom had been riding Sable.

The tent had large flaps that opened up along the entire front, so that all the exhibits could be shown nicely to the people in the seats outside.

The seats were made of boards set on almost anything that could hold them, with a few garden benches for reserved seats at the front.

The circus day came at last, and everything was ready.

"Lucky it isn't raining," Bert declared, as the boys rushed around putting the final touches to everything.

August Stout was appointed to collect the tickets, and Ned Prentice was to show the people to their seats.

Two o'clock!

Only one hour more!

Lots of children came early to get good seats. Roy Mason sat right in the front row alongside Freddie. Nettie Prentice was on the very first bench behind the reserved seats. The Herolds came next, and had Aunt Sarah's front garden bench, the red one. Mildred Manners' mother and father paid twenty-five cents each, too, and they had the big green bench from the side porch.

"Give Mrs. Burns a front seat," Harry whispered to Ned. The busy farmer's wife actually had stopped her work to come and see what all the excitement was about.

Everyone from the Bobbsey farm had come, except John—someone had to stay home to take care of things. Dinah, in a big red hat, was all smiles.

"When will it begin?" Flossie asked, trembling with excitement.

"I saw Harry and Bert go in the tent some time ago," whispered Nan. "And see, they're loosening the tent flap."

There was a shout of applause when Harry appeared. He wore a swallow-tailed coat which was much too big for him. The sleeves were turned up twice, and the back touched the ground. He wore a very high collar which was so stiff he could hardly turn his head. A bright green tie completed the costume.

Aunt Sarah had to smile when she saw him; her son looked so funny. There was a ripple of laughter as the audience looked at him, but in a moment it turned to one of admiration for the show.

"Oh!" exclaimed all the children, when they looked inside the tent.

"Isn't it grand!" whispered Flossie.

Next Bert appeared and stepped up on a soap box in the middle of the tent.

"Ladies and gentlemen," he began, making a low bow, "ladies and gentlemen——"

His hat tumbled off. As he stooped to pick it up, the children giggled. Realizing that he was amusing them, Bert put the hat back on and bowed and said, "Ladies and gentlemen," and let the hat fall off again. Even the grown-ups got to laughing.

Bert was dressed a good deal like Harry, except that Bert wore a red tie. Presently he waved his hand at the audience for silence.

"Ladies and gentlemen! Our first number is Frisky, the Sacred Calf of India!" he exclaimed, imitating that hoarse-voiced man called a "barker" who works at circuses.

Snap, snap! went Bert's whip, and everyone watched to see what would happen.

CHAPTER XIV

THE CHARIOT RACE

OUT from the side, behind a big screen, came Jack Hopkins, dressed like a clown, leading Frisky, the runaway calf.

Over the calf was a red velvet cape that reached clear down to the ground, and over each ear was tied a long-handled feather duster! Such laughing and clapping as greeted this "first number"!

Frisky stopped walking and looked the people straight in the face. This funny move made Mr. Bobbsey almost "die laughing", as Flossie said, and Uncle Daniel, too, was hilarious.

"The sacred calf is too sacred to smile," he said, while Dinah and Martha just roared.

Suddenly, Jack, the clown, jumped on the calf's back. He tried to stand on his head. Then he turned a somersault, ending up gracefully on the ground.

Next he came around and kissed Frisky. This

made everybody roar again. In fact, no matter what the clown did, it looked so very funny that it set the crowd laughing. Finally, Bert snapped his whip three times, and Jack jumped on Frisky's back, and rode off.

"I really never enjoyed a big circus more than this!" remarked Mrs. Bobbsey to Mrs. Burns.

Then Bert announced the next event. "Ladies and gentlemen," he continued, "our next number will introduce to you the famous wildcats, Snoop and Fluffy. Real wildcats from the jungle, and this is the first—time—they—have ever been— exhibited in—this country!"

Snap went the whip, and out came Harry with Snoop and Fluffy, the kittens, one on each arm.

He whistled, and Snoop climbed on his shoulder!

This "brought the house down", as Uncle Daniel later described the applause, and there was so much noise that the kittens looked frightened.

Next Harry stretched out both arms straight in front of him, and the kittens carefully walked over into his hands.

"Well, I declare!" exclaimed Dinah. "Just see that Snoop kitty!"

Harry stooped down and let the kittens jump through his hands, an old but very pretty trick.

With the air of a real ringmaster, Bert snapped

his whip. On a table he placed a little block of
wood, and on top of that a short board. He
rubbed something on each end. It was a bit of
dried herring, but the people did not know that.
Then Harry put Snoop on one end of the board
and Fluffy on the other.

"Oh, a seesaw!" called Freddie, unable to
restrain his joy any longer. "I bet on Snoop.
He's heavier'n Fluffy."

At the sound of Freddie's voice, Snoop turned
around. The move sent Fluffy right up in the
air.

"Oh! Oh! Oh!" came a chorus from the
children, but before anybody in the circus had
time to interfere, off went Fluffy, as hard as she
could run, over the fields for home.

The next minute Snoop was after her, and
Harry stood alone in the ring, bowing. When the
tremendous applause ceased, Bert made the next
announcement.

"Ladies and gentlemen," he said, "we will now
introduce our famous menagerie. First we have
the singing mice."

"They're mine!" called Freddie, but Nan
shushed him quickly.

"Listen and you will hear the mice sing," said
Bert. As he held up the cage of little mice, somebody whistled a funny tune behind the scenes.

"Good! Good!" called Mr. Bobbsey. "We have real talent here," he added, for indeed the boys had put together a fine show.

"Now you shall see our aquarium," continued Bert as Harry helped him bring forward the table that held the glass tank. "Here we have a real sea-serpent," he said, pointing to a good fat chub that flopped around in the water.

"Now here are our alligators and crocodiles," announced Bert, pointing his whip at the turtles. "And these are sea lions," he said, meaning the giant frogs. Freddie's hoptoads were called baby kangaroos from Australia!

At each announcement everybody laughed, but Bert went on as seriously as if everything were true.

"In this separate tank," he declared, "we have our boa constrictors, the largest and fiercest snakes in the world."

Jack's snakes were the ones that came in for this description, and the girls were a bit afraid of them, although the snakes were in a glass jar and could not get out.

"Now," said Bert, "here are crystal fish from the deep sea!" These were Tom's goldfish. "You will notice how bespangled they are. I'm told this comes from the fish eating the diamonds lost in shipwrecks."

"What a story!" called someone behind the scenes whose voice sounded like Tom Mason's.

Snap! went Bert's whip, and the boys did not interrupt him again.

"The last part of our menagerie is the cage of prize butterflies," said Bert. "These butterflies are rare and scarce and——"

"Hard to catch!" remarked Nan.

"Now there will be ten minutes' intermission," said Ringmaster Bobbsey, "so you may have time to see everything in the menagerie."

"After that we will give you the best number on the programme, our chariot race."

During the intermission August sold a big basket of peanuts, and the people wanted more. They knew all the money was to go to the fresh air camp, which probably was the reason they bought so generously.

All this time there was plenty of noise behind the scenes, and it was evident something big was being prepared. Presently Bert and Harry came out and lowered the tent flap, first making sure all the sightseers were outside.

"They're coming!" exclaimed Freddie, clapping his chubby hands.

"Now, ladies and gentlemen," called Tom Mason, appearing at the tent, "if you will just turn around the other way in your seats and face that riding ring we will give you an exhibition of cowboy life on the plains!"

Tom's costume was perfect; he had received it only the Hallowe'en before. After bowing, he went behind the scenes a moment, then returned riding the fiery Sable. The colt was bridled and saddled.

Bert stepped into the middle of the riding ring alongside some boxes that were piled up there. Tapping them, he announced:

"Ladies and gentlemen, this is a mail coach." He laughed in spite of himself. "Our cowboy will rob the mail coach from his horse just as they used to do long ago in the mountains out West."

He cracked the whip, and away went Sable around the ring at a nice canter. After a few laps, Tom urged his horse on until he was going at a steady run. Everyone kept quiet, for most of Meadow Brook's people had heard how Sable had run away some days before.

"This is the mail," Bert announced, laying Harry's canvas schoolbag stuffed full of papers on the boxes. "The coach has stopped for a few minutes."

Crack! Crack! went the whip as the colt ran faster and faster. All of a sudden Tom got a good tight hold on the reins, stood up in the stirrups, and pulled up alongside the mail coach. He leaned over, grabbed the mailbag, and turned his colt full speed around the riding ring.

"Hurrah! Hurrah!" shouted everybody.

"Well done!" called Uncle Daniel.

Tom waved his hat now and patted Sable affectionately, as all good riders do when their horses have done well in a show.

"One more number," called Bert. "The chariot race."

Out came two goats, pulling wagons that had high cardboard fronts and sides like chariots. Standing in the chariots were Jack and August. They had on white robes and bands across their foreheads like Roman charioteers of long ago.

"One, two, three!" called Bert, holding a cap pistol up in the air. "Ready! Set! Go!"

Bang! went the cap pistol and away started the chariots.

Jack wore a broad green belt and August wore a yellow one. Jack darted ahead!

"Go it, green!" shouted Harry.

"Pass him, yellow!" called Tom.

Finally August passed Jack just as they crossed the line.

"One!" called Bert. "We will have five heats."

In the next race the wagons kept almost even until just within a few feet of the line, then Jack crossed first.

"Two!" called Bert, while all the boys shouted for their favourites.

In the next two turns the riders divided evenly. Now the last round was reached and the score was tied. This, of course, made the race very exciting, as both had an equal chance of winning.

Bang went the pistol! Off went the chariots!

"Come on, green!"

"Come on, yellow!"

Shout after shout greeted the riders as they urged their steeds around the ring.

Suddenly Jack's chariot crossed in front of August.

"Foul!" called Bert, while Jack tried his best to get on his own side again.

"Back! Back!" yelled Jack to his goat, but the little animal was too excited to obey.

Finally August Stout, wearing the yellow belt, dashed home first and won the race!

"Good for you!" "Swell!" "Congratulations!" said children and grown-ups.

"Hurrah! Hurrah! Hurrah!" shouted the boys long and loud.

The circus was over!

The money was counted, and there were exactly fifty-seven dollars and twenty-five cents, for many had put in bills instead of quarters, to be given to the Meadow Brook Fresh Air Camp for city children.

"Wasn't that splendid?" said Aunt Sarah Bobbsey. "Everybody had such a good time!"

A committee of five boys, Bert, Harry, Jack, Tom, and August, took the money over to the fresh air camp the next day. The director said it was a very welcome gift, for the money would enable at least five children, who otherwise would not be able to leave the hot city, to spend a week in the country.

For some days every boy and girl in Meadow Brook talked about the circus, which had really been a greater success than even the boys themselves had expected.

One warm afternoon late in July—one of those days that makes a boy feel lazy—the Bobbsey boys had a visit from Mark Teron. He had been on his good behaviour for some time now, and had even helped with the circus. So when he wanted to play with Bert and Harry, they let him, and the three boys went down behind the barn together.

They played jack-knife awhile, sitting down on a stack of hay that John had just dropped there. John was bringing loads from a field and putting them in the barn. Part of the top of the last load had been brushed off at the door.

"Say, did you fellows ever try smoking?" Mark asked suddenly.

"No!" answered Bert in surprise. "Dad wouldn't let me smoke."

"Neither would my pop," said Harry.

"Listen," said Mark, "every fellow tries it sometime. I've seen them make cigarettes out of corn silk."

"I suppose that's not as bad as tobacco," replied Bert.

"No," answered Mark, "there's no harm in corn silk. I'll show you how to roll a cigarette if you can find some corn silk."

At this Harry slid down off the hay and went to the corncrib. After looking a few minutes, he found some withered black strands on the floor and carried them to Mark.

"I need some soft paper to put around it," said Mark.

Harry found some in a tool chest. He and Bert watched with interest as Mark made a clumsy looking cigarette.

"There!" he exclaimed. "How is that?"

"Pretty good," answered Bert. "Looks just like a real one."

"Let's try it!" Mark proposed, pulling a match from his pocket, and lighting it.

"Kind of strong," he spluttered. "You try it!"

Bert put the cigarette in his mouth. He drew on it once, then quickly handed it to Harry.

"Ugh!" he exclaimed. "Tastes like old shoes!"

Harry did not like it any better than Bert had.

"My mouth feels like a stove," he said, coughing. "One that needs cleaning."

He gave it back to Mark, who puffed on it several times, pretending to enjoy it. But the other boys could see he did not like the taste of it any better than they had. Suddenly he exclaimed:

"Oh gee!" He had seen John walking toward the barn.

Mark quickly pushed the cigarette into the ground, shoved some hay over it, and took to his heels. Bert and Harry looked sheepish. But John did not seem to notice anything wrong. If he did, he said nothing on the subject of smoking.

"How about you fellows helping me with the hay?" he asked. "A storm's coming up. It'll spoil the hay."

"Sure, we'll help," they chorused.

With this the two boys started at a run down through the fields into the open meadow, where the sweet-smelling hay was being pitched into the hay wagon. Betty and Billy stood waiting, as they flicked flies with their long tails.

John, of course, was very glad of the help, for

rain spoils hay. All three worked hard to load up before the heavy shower came down.

"All ready!" called John presently, climbing up to the driver's seat. "And no time to lose."

The boys hopped on and John started for the barn. As they neared it, John cried, horrified:

"The barn is on fire!"

CHAPTER XV

THE FLOOD

JOHN almost fell from his seat on the wagon in his haste to get down.

Bert and Harry were so frightened they could hardly move. They knew they were to blame. The cigarette had not been properly put out!

"The hose!" called John, seeing flames now shoot out of the barn windows. "Get the hose, Harry! Hurry! Bert, tell Mr. Bobbsey to call the fire station!" and Bert raced off.

Near the barn stood an iron framework with a tower on top, which caught and stored rain water for just such an emergency. Almost immediately everybody came running out of the house except Uncle Daniel, who was telephoning.

"Oh, how dreadful!" cried Aunt Sarah. "The whole barn will go."

Uncle Daniel soon arrived and began to pour

water on the flames, which had spread from the blazing haystack to the rear of the barn.

"Get the animals out!" he shouted to John.

"Where are the firemen?" cried Freddie. "Get the firemen!"

"They're coming from Meadow Brook," said Nan. "But the barn'll burn up before they can get here. We'll have to put it out ourselves."

Freddie burst into tears. He loved the old barn. The little boy suddenly realized that playing fireman and really trying to put out a bad fire were two different things. Oh, why didn't the fire brigade come?

Two fire extinguishers, the farm hose, and the buckets of water seemed to be doing no good at all. The flames were making rapid headway.

All this time the thunderstorm, which everyone had forgotten, was now approaching swiftly. Clap after clap of thunder rolled over the hills and the fire looked even more terrible against the black sky.

"The rain!" exclaimed Uncle Daniel suddenly. "The rain may put out the fire. We can't. All the water's gone from the tank!"

Just as he spoke, the downpour started. A high wind sent a deluge of water right through the wide open door and into the barn. As it fell on the flames, it sent up clouds of hissing steam, but it helped to keep the fire from spreading.

In the midst of this a fire-engine came clanging down the lane, and within ten minutes the fire was out. The barn had been saved!

"How did it start?" the firemen asked.

"I have no idea," Uncle Daniel answered, puzzled.

Bert and Harry were pale and trembling. They said nothing, but late that afternoon the two of them spoke to Harry's father alone.

"Pop," said Harry, tears in his eyes, "it was our fault the barn caught fire!"

"What!" exclaimed Uncle Daniel. "You boys set the barn afire?"

Together the boys told the story of the corn-silk cigarette, but they did not mention Mark's name.

"Cigarette!" Uncle Daniel thundered. "You boys smoking!"

Both Bert and Harry started to cry. There was no conversation for a couple of minutes, then Uncle Daniel said:

"Boys, this has been a serious lesson to you, I hope, and one which you will remember all your lives. I need not punish you; you have suffered enough from the fright of that awful fire. And if you had refused to go along with the schemes of that young scamp, whoever he was, this whole thing wouldn't have happened."

"I'll never listen to anybody again who tries to make me do something wrong," Harry declared.

"Me either," Bert promised.

"I'm sure you mean that," answered Uncle Daniel, "and we'll say no more about it."

This ended the boys' confession, but they felt so sick and nervous that they went to bed without eating any supper.

Next day it rained very hard—in fact, it was one of those cold, blustery storms that came once every summer to Meadow Brook and lasted and lasted.

"The gate at the dam is closed," Aunt Sarah reported to the others, after talking to a neighbour on the telephone. "And if the pond gets any higher, they won't be able to cross the plank to open up the gate and let the water out."

"That would be dangerous, wouldn't it?" asked Nan.

"Very," replied her aunt. "Peter Burns's house is just below the dam at the other side of the outlet. If the dam should ever burst, his house would be swept away."

"And his barn and hen-house are even nearer than the house!" Uncle Daniel remarked. "It would be a terrible loss for him."

"Let's go up in the attic. We may be able to see from there how high the pond is," Aunt Sarah suggested, after Uncle Daniel and the older boys went off to see if they could do anything for the Burnses.

From the top floor of the house the Bobbseys could see across the high pond bank and get a good view of the water.

"Oh," Nan exclaimed. "Isn't it awful! That's not all rain water, is it?"

"A good deal of it," her aunt replied. "You see, all the streams from the mountains drain into this pond, and in a big storm like this it is filled to overflowing."

"Why do people build houses in such dangerous places?" asked Nan.

"Well, you see, the Burns' house has stood there more than two hundred years—long before any dam was put in the pond to work the saw-mill," said Aunt Sarah. "And now even the saw-mill's not used any more."

"Oh, that's it—is it?" said the twins' mother. "I thought it was peculiar to put houses right below a dam."

"See how strong the current is getting," remarked Aunt Sarah. "Look at that big log floating down."

"It will be fun when it stops raining," remarked

Freddie. "We can sail things almost any-where."

This gave Freddie an idea and he went down the cellar at once. Soon he was hammering. Flossie and Nan ran to see what their brother was doing.

"Hey!" called Freddie from the floor. "Bring me some more nails, will you? I need them for my ark."

"An ark!" laughed Nan. "I guess we'll need it all right if this storm keeps on."

She got some nails from a tool-box and handed them to her little brother.

"How's that?" he asked, standing the raft up on end.

"I guess that will float," said Nan, "and when it stops raining, we can try it."

"I'm going to make a regular ark like the play one I've got at home," said Freddie, "only mine will be a big one with room for us all, and even Frisky and Snoop and Fluffy besides."

Freddie went on working as seriously as if he really expected to be a little Noah and save all the people from the flood.

"My, but it sure is raining!" exclaimed some-body on the front porch.

It was Uncle Daniel, who had just returned from the village with Bert and Harry. They were soaking wet.

"It's too late to open the gate," Uncle Daniel announced. "They let the water get so high the plank's sailed away, and now they can't get near the dam."

"Why don't they go to the gate in a boat?" asked Nan.

"Why, my dear girl," said Uncle Daniel, "anybody who went near that torrent in a boat might as well jump off the bridge. The dam is fifteen feet high, and the water pouring over it now must be several feet deep. If anyone should go within two hundred feet of the dam, the surging water would carry him over."

"You see," said Harry, explaining it further, "there is something like a window in the dam, a long, low door. When this is opened, the water is drawn down under, and does not have to go over the falls."

"And if there is too much pressure against the stone wall that makes the dam, the wall may be carried away. That's what we mean when we say the dam's bursting," finished Uncle Daniel.

"I had better have John bring the Burns family up here," said Aunt Sarah, worried.

"I stopped in on my way up," Uncle Daniel told her, "and they are ready to move out at a moment's notice. We'll bring them up here if it gets any worse."

It was an anxious night in Meadow Brook, and few people went to bed. The men took turns walking along the bank of the pond all night, and their shouts above the steady roar of the water pouring over the dam made the situation even more frightening.

The men carried lanterns and flashlights, and the little specks of light were all that could be seen through the darkness.

Mrs. Burns had refused to leave her home. "I will stay as long as I can," she told Uncle Daniel, who had come down with Bert and Harry to be of help if necessary. "I have lived here many a year, and that dam has not broken yet, so I'm not going to give up hope now!"

"But you could hardly get out in time if it should break," insisted Uncle Daniel, "and you know we have plenty of room and you are welcome to visit us."

Still she insisted upon staying. Peter, of course, was out with the men. He could not move his barns and hen-house, but he had taken his cow and horse to places of safety. The Bobbseys offered to carry some suitcases of clothes back to their home, in case it became necessary to move out quickly.

There were other families along the road in danger as well as the Burnses, but they were not so near the dam, and would get more warning before the flood could reach them, should the dam burst.

How the water roared! And how awfully dark it was! Would morning never come?

"Four o'clock—the water is still rising!" shouted the men from the bank.

"Mary!" called Peter Burns at the door of their little home, "put on your raincoat and go with the boys as fast as you can! Don't wait to take anything, but go!"

"Oh, my babies' pictures!" she cried. "My dear babies! I must have them."

The poor frightened little woman rushed about the house looking for the much-prized pictures of her children who had died in their childhood so many years before.

"It's a good thing my darlings both have a safe home tonight," she thought.

"Come, Mary!" called Peter outside. "The dam is beginning to bulge in the middle. She'll go any minute." With one last look at her home, Mrs. Burns went out and closed the door.

Outside there were people from all along the road, some driven out of their homes in alarm, others having turned out to help their neighbours.

The watchmen had left the bank. A torrent from the dam would surely wash that away, and brave as the men were, they could not watch the flood any longer.

"Get past the willows, quick!" called one of them. "Let everybody who is not needed hurry up the road!"

"What's that?" called Uncle Daniel, as there was a heavy crash over near the gate.

Everybody listened, breathless. Daylight was just breaking, and they could see the dam was still there.

"It's pretty strong!" said the watchman. "I expected to hear it crash an hour ago!"

There was another crash!

"There she goes!" said Mr. Burns, and then nobody spoke.

CHAPTER XVI

A TOWN AFLOAT

"DID the dam really burst?" asked Uncle Daniel after a wait of several minutes, during which no extra water came pouring down.

"I'll go up to the pipes and look," volunteered John. "I can see from there."

"Be careful," Uncle Daniel warned.

Now the pipes were great water conduits, the immense black iron kind that are used for carrying water into cities from reservoirs. They were situated some distance above the dam, but John could see the gate as he stood on the pipes.

"What's that?" he thought, as he looked down the raging stream. "Something is jammed across the dam!" he shouted to the anxious listeners.

This was enough. In another minute every man was on the pond bank.

"The big elm!" they shouted. "It has saved the dam!"

131

What a wonderful thing had happened! The giant elm tree that for so many years had stood on the edge of the stream just opposite the dam, had crashed, its roots weakened by the flood. Its hundred and fifty feet lay braced against the centre of the dam, reinforcing it at its most threatened point. The old dam was saved!

"We're safe now, thank heavens!" exclaimed Uncle Daniel. "It was the tree we heard crash against the dam. The storm has let up at last, and that tree will hold where it is stuck until the water goes down."

To think that all the houses in Meadow Brook had been spared! And the Burnses could come back to their old mill home once more!

"We must never run this risk again," said Uncle Daniel to Mr. Mason. "When the water goes down we will open the gate. Then when the next dry spell comes and there is little water in the pond, we will break down the dam and just let the river run through without the falls."

Early the next morning the Bobbseys learned that though a real disaster had been averted, there was a good deal of land under water.

"Hey, Bert and Harry!" called Tom Mason, as he and Jack Hopkins ran past the Bobbsey place on their way to see the damage. "Come on down and see the flood."

The boys did not wait for breakfast but, with a buttered roll in each hand, Harry and Bert joined the others and hurried off toward the town.

"Look at this," called Tom, as they came to a turn in the road where the water covered it completely.

"We'll have to walk on the fence to get across," said Bert.

"Or else get a boat," grinned Harry. "Say, maybe Herold's boat is still tied up."

The boys sloshed through a field to the pond. Herold's rowboat was tied to a tree.

"Let's borrow it for a little while," said Jack.

"You fellows get in, and I'll push off," said Harry.

The other three climbed in, then Harry gave a good push and scrambled over the edge himself.

"Think of rowing a boat in the middle of a street," said Bert, as they reached the road again. "That's the way they do in Venice," he added, "but I never expected to see such a thing in Meadow Brook."

The boys rowed along quite easily, as the water was quite deep enough. Soon they had rounded the curve of the road and were crossing a flooded field below the dam near the Burns' farm.

"Oh look!" called Bert. "There goes the Burns' hen-house."

Sure enough, the hen-house had left its foundation and was now floating down the river on its roof. There were at least fifty chickens and some ducks in it. Now they were fluttering about in the upturned house.

"Maybe we can save 'em for Mr. Burns," cried Harry, rowing faster.

The chickens made an awful noise as they tried to keep on the floating house! The ducks soon flew off and landed quacking on the water, enjoying themselves immensely.

"We ought to have a rope to pull the house in," said Tom.

"Where are we going to find a rope?" scoffed Jack.

Bert suddenly had an idea. He lifted up the lid of the bait box, and sure enough, there lay a rope. By splicing this to the tow rope, it was long enough to work with.

"Push up closer to the house, Harry," said Bert, as he looped the end of the rope.

Then he threw it, once, twice—the third time it caught on a corner of the hen-house. He pulled the knot tight, and the floating house was secure.

"Hurrah! Hurrah!" shouted the other boys.

"Don't pull too hard!" warned Harry suddenly. "You'll upset the boat."

All this time the chickens were cackling and

screeching, as the house in the water lunged from one side to the other. Finally Bert, with the other boys' help, dragged it to dry land. Several men who had seen the rescue, including Harry's father, ran over to them.

"We may as well finish the job," said Uncle Daniel. "Harry, go hitch Billy and Betty up to the big cart and we'll take the hen-house back to Peter, only this time we'll put it on higher ground."

By running across the fields that bordered the unflooded section of the road, Harry was able to get home quickly, and soon returned with the cart and team.

It took many willing hands to get the hen-house on the cart, but this was finally done, and away went Billy and Betty through the water with the queer load after them. The chickens had been captured and put into crates.

There were many sights to be seen about Meadow Brook that afternoon, and the boys did not miss any of them. In one of the village streets Bert caught a big catfish and a black-spotted lizard that had been flooded out from some dark place in the mountains.

Harry found a pretty toy canoe that some small boy probably had been playing with in the stream before the water rose, and gave it to Freddie.

Freddie had boots on, and was happy sailing both the new boat and his ark up and down a small new pond that the rain had made on the farm. He insisted upon trying to take Snoop for a ride. But cats do not fancy water and the black kitten quickly ran off and hid himself up in the hayloft, out of Freddie's reach.

When the water subsided a few days later, Nan and Flossie went for a walk with their mother and Aunt Sarah. The hot July sun had dried up large areas. Many vegetable gardens were gone, hay was rotting, and many small wild animals had been drowned.

This loss, however, was nothing compared with what had been expected by the farmers, and all were satisfied that only a kind Providence had saved the valley houses from complete destruction.

Nan's vegetable garden had received a dreadful soaking, and it took her days to coax the lettuce, cabbage, broccoli, and carrot tops to an upright position. While she was working in the garden one morning, Mildred Manners came over.

"Oh, what do you think?" she said. "Part of the fresh air camp was flooded. The children lost some of their clothes, and—and a lot of them caught cold and are real sick."

"That's too bad," said Nan soberly. "Maybe we can do something for them."

The two girls ran to find Mrs. Bobbsey and Aunt Sarah. After hearing the story, the twins' mother suggested they all drive over to the camp and find out what was needed.

"We'll go this afternoon right after dinner," said Aunt Sarah.

"I want to go too," Freddie spoke up, hearing the plans at the dinner table about going to the fresh air camp.

"Me, too," said Flossie eagerly, bouncing in her chair.

"We'll take the station wagon," said Aunt Sarah, "then we can all go."

So that was how the Bobbseys became interested again in the fresh air camp. Nan and Mildred, Flossie and Freddie, with Aunt Sarah and Mrs. Bobbsey, visited the camp at three o'clock.

"It's all white tents," whispered Flossie, as they drove up to the camp along the river.

"Oh, this is like a soldier camp!" exclaimed Freddie, when he saw the tents. "They're just like the war pictures in my story-book!"

Mrs. Manily, who had charge of the camp, came up, and when Mrs. Bobbsey explained their errand, the director was pleased to learn of their sympathy.

"Those were your boys who brought us all that money from the circus, weren't they?" she asked.

"I'm glad the boys were able to help," said Mrs. Bobbsey. "It really was quite a circus."

"It must have been, to have made so much money," Mrs. Manily replied.

"And we are going to help now," spoke up Nan. "Please tell us what we can do."

CHAPTER XVII

VISITING CAMP

MRS. MANILY thought the greatest need in camp was clothes to replace the ones the flood had ruined. But such an expense would be out of the question, she added.

"We can soon solve that," Mrs. Bobbsey smiled. "If we make them, we can keep the expense down."

"I can sew," Nan spoke up. "Can you, Mildred?"

Mildred nodded. Her grandmother had taught her how to knit and sew, she said. Also, several other girls who went to school with her could sew well.

"We'll have a sewing class," declared Nan, "and we'll make lots of clothes."

"You're sweet girls," said Mrs. Manily, delighted with the idea. "And now, would you like to look around the camp?"

All the visitors wanted to, so she took them outside. By this time several small boys and girls had come up. Mrs. Manily introduced them.

Nan and Mildred made friends with some of the girls, while Freddie and Flossie soon were giggling with the little boys. One boy, smaller than Freddie, with sandy hair and beautiful blue eyes, was particularly taken with Freddie. He was almost as fat as Freddie, and his skin was tanned and clear.

"Where do you live?" he asked Freddie.

"At Uncle Daniel's, and sometimes at my own house," Freddie answered. "Do you have two homes?"

"No, I just live with Mrs. Manily, 'cause my mummy's gone far, far away. Can I come over and play with you?" he asked. "What's your name?"

Flossie answered before Freddie could open his mouth. "His name is Freddie and mine is Flossie. What's your name?"

"Mine is Edward Brooks," said the little camper, "but everybody calls me Sandy. Do you like Sandy better than Edward?"

"No," replied Flossie. "But I suppose that's a pet name because your hair is that colour."

"Is it?" said the boy, instinctively putting his hand to his close-cropped head. "Maybe that's why, then!"

"Guess it is," said Freddie. "But will Mrs. Man let you come over to our house?"

"Mrs. Manily, you mean," said Sandy. "I'll go and ask her."

"I'm going to ask Mummy if we can bring him home to stay," declared Freddie as Sandy ran off in search of Mrs. Manily. "He could sleep in my bed."

The others of the party were now walking along the row of tents.

"This is where we eat," the director explained, as they entered a huge canvas pavilion.

The tent was filled with long narrow tables and benches. The tables were covered with oilcloth, and in the centre of each was a beautiful bunch of fresh wild flowers—small, pretty ones which the children had gathered in the woods.

"You ought to see our children eat," remarked Mrs. Manily. "We have all we can do to serve them, they have such good appetites from the country air."

"We must send you some fresh vegetables," said Aunt Sarah, "and some fruit."

"We would be very grateful," replied Mrs. Manily, "for of course we cannot afford much of a variety."

Next to the dining-room was the smallest boys' sleeping tent.

"We have a little boys' drum corps," said the director, "and every pleasant evening they march around with drums and tin fifes. Then, when it is bedtime, we have a boy blow 'taps' on a tin bugle."

In the tent were four rows of small white cots. They looked very clean and comfortable, and the end of this tent was closed with a big green mosquito netting.

"How old are your smallest children?" Aunt Sarah asked Mrs. Manily.

"Sandy is our baby," replied the director, patting the little boy fondly, "and he is just five years old."

"Then he's younger than Freddie," said Mrs. Bobbsey. "What a dear sweet child Sandy is!"

"Yes," whispered Mrs. Manily, "he has just lost his mother, and his father cannot care for him—that is, he cannot afford to pay his board or hire a housekeeper, so he brought him to the Children's Aid Society. He is the pet of the camp."

"No mother and no home!" sighed Mrs. Bobbsey. "Poor little boy!" she thought. "Imagine my Freddie being alone like that!"

Mrs. Bobbsey, tears in her eyes, stooped over and kissed Sandy.

"Do you know my mummy?" he asked, looking straight into her kind face.

"Mrs. Manily is your mummy now, isn't she?" said Mrs. Bobbsey.

"Yes, she's my number-two mummy, but I mean the one that used to let me bounce on her bed in the morning."

"Come now, Sandy," smiled Mrs. Manily. "Didn't you tell me last night I was the best mummy in the whole world?" And she hugged the little fellow to make him happy again.

"Yes," he laughed, forgetting all his loneliness now. "When I get to be a big man, I'm goin' to take you for an aeroplane ride."

"Can Sandy come home with us?" Freddie asked his mother. "He can sleep in my bed."

"You are very kind," said the director. "But we cannot let any of our children go visiting without special permission from the Society."

"Well," said Aunt Sarah, "if you get the permission, we will be very glad to have Sandy pay us a visit. We have plenty of room and we would really enjoy having him."

"Oh, let him come now," pleaded Freddie, not understanding about the rules. "See, we have room in the station wagon."

"Well, he might have a ride," consented Mrs. Manily, and before anyone had a chance to speak again, Freddie and Sandy had climbed into the front seat.

Nan and Mildred had been talking to some of the older girls, and Nan declared that she was coming over to the camp to play with them soon for a whole day.

"We can bring our lunch," said Mildred, "and you can show us all the nice play places you have found on the mountainside."

One girl, named Connie, was taller than the others and very pale. She brought Mrs. Bobbsey a bunch of wild flowers she had just gathered.

"What a lovely gift, my dear," exclaimed Mrs. Bobbsey, stooping to kiss the shy little girl on the cheek.

"This is Connie McLaughlin, Mrs. Bobbsey," said Mrs. Manily. "This is her first summer with us. She hasn't been very well, but she's better now."

"Do you like camping, Connie?" inquired Aunt Sarah.

"Oh, I love it," replied Connie. "I wish I didn't ever have to leave."

On the way back to the car Mrs. Manily whispered to Mrs. Bobbsey and Aunt Sarah that Connie's visit would soon be over. How she wished the frail child might stay longer, until she had regained her full strength!

When the women reached the car, Flossie had already climbed in with Sandy and Freddie.

"Can't Connie come for a little ride, too?" asked Nan. "There is plenty of room."

Mrs. Manily said yes, and so the little group started off for a ride along the road toward Meadow Brook.

"I was never in a car before in all my life," said Connie suddenly. "I feel as though I were flying through the air!"

"Never?" exclaimed the other girls in surprise.

"No," said Connie. "I've had lots of rides in buses, and we had a ride in a farm wagon the other day, but this is the first time I have ever been in a car like this."

Aunt Sarah was letting Sandy sit beside her and put his hands on the steering wheel. The little boy was delighted. Freddie enjoyed it almost as well as Sandy did, and kept telling him which way to turn the wheel. Of course, Aunt Sarah's hands never left the wheel, but Sandy was firmly convinced he was doing the steering.

"We'll stop at Smith's Milk Bar and have some ice-cream," said Mrs. Bobbsey.

This was good news to everybody. When they walked inside the little hillside eating place, who should be sitting there enjoying ice-cream but Bert and Harry Bobbsey!

"Hallo!" they called, getting up.

Nan introduced Connie and Sandy, then every-one ordered his favourite flavour of ice-cream. Freddie and Sandy finished theirs first and went outside.

They were so eager to start off that they jumped into the driver's seat of the station wagon before the others were ready to go. Then, either by accident or just because he was an inquisitive little boy, Sandy released the emergency brake!

At once the station wagon began to roll slowly down the hill with no one in it but Sandy and Freddie!

CHAPTER XVIII

THE THIMBLE BRIGADE

SEEING the car move with only Freddie and Sandy in it, Bert and Harry raced outside. They started running after the station wagon as fast as they could.

"Put on the brake!" shouted Harry. "Put on the brake!"

But Sandy, who was in the driver's seat, was so excited he merely kept twisting the steering wheel to right and left, which, of course, made the car swerve crazily from one side of the road to the other.

Bert and Harry knew that if the car should go much faster, there would be a bad accident. At this point the road was level with the open fields on both sides. If the car would only turn into one of them, it might stop.

"Steer into the field!" screamed Bert.

Freddie heard him. Though he was almost too

frightened to obey, he did take hold of the wheel and pull it hard to the right.

The other Bobbseys, who had come out of the eating place, cried out in alarm.

"They'll go in a ditch and overturn!" wailed Aunt Sarah.

"Oh! Oh! Oh!" screamed Nan, for the car was now bumping across the ditch and into a field.

At that moment a lucky twist of the steering wheel sent the station wagon head on into a large haystack. The car stopped and the haystack collapsed, festooning the station wagon with hay.

The next minute Bert and Harry were at the car beside Sandy and Freddie.

"Are you all right?" they asked.

Freddie was just rising from the floor, rubbing his head, which he had bumped against a door. Sandy was holding his stomach, which had hit the steering wheel hard. Both little boys started to cry.

Bert and Harry lifted them out, and carried them to the road. Mrs. Bobbsey and the others had reached the scene by this time. Such cuddling as Freddie and Sandy got! Everyone was relieved that they had not been badly injured. Sandy had had no idea of making the car run away, so no one scolded him. But the little boy had another worry. Maybe now he would not be allowed to visit the Bobbseys!

The twins' mother said she would speak to Mrs. Manily about this when they got back to the camp. She was sure Sandy would be more careful in the future.

"I'll never, never touch anything in a car again, till I'm a big boy and can drive," Sandy promised.

A short time later, when they reached the camp, he told the director the same thing, and then begged her to let him visit the Bobbseys.

"Well, we'll see," Mrs. Manily answered. "I can't tell you now."

As the Bobbseys started away, she and Sandy and Connie waved until the car was out of sight.

"I just love Connie," said Nan a few minutes later. "I wish she wasn't so weak."

"Weak?" asked the twins' mother.

Nan said that Connie often fainted because she was not strong. And she could not play games like the other children.

"I'm sure that with good food and rest she'll be better," said Mrs. Bobbsey. "And now, I think we had better decide what our sewing class is going to make for the camp children."

"I'd like to make a pretty playsuit," Mildred spoke up.

"Boys don't wear playsuits," scoffed Freddie.

"I'll get some strong material and make the boys overalls," declared Aunt Sarah.

"Red ones," said Freddie, "like my fireman's suit."

It was decided that next morning the two Mrs. Bobbseys would go shopping in Meadow Brook and buy some materials. Nan and Mildred telephoned their other friends that evening, and they promised to come to the Bobbsey farm at two o'clock the following afternoon to help sew.

"What pretty material!" exclaimed Mabel when she arrived the next day. She was the first one to come.

"It's for playsuits," Nan told her. "And that green-and-white stripe over there is for pyjamas, and this blue is for overalls."

Mabel giggled. "Give me something easy to make. I can't sew very well!"

By two o'clock the sewing class was ready to go into action. Aunt Sarah had turned a big attic room into a sewing-room. Flossie was to look after the spools of thread, keeping them from becoming tangled, and the girls agreed to let Freddie help cut paper patterns.

This was not a play sewing class but a real one, for Aunt Sarah and Mrs. Bobbsey were to do the machine work, while the girls were to do the basting and sew on the buttons.

Besides Mabel, Mildred, Nan, and Nettie, there were Marie Brenn, who was visiting the Herolds, Bessie, and Anna Thomas, a big girl who lived over near Hillside. Each one had brought her own little sewing kit with thimble, needles, and scissors.

Immediately the girls began to follow Mrs. Bobbsey's instructions, and very soon all the frills were ready for the machine. Nan handed them to her mother, and then Aunt Sarah gave out some work.

"Now these are the pockets," said Aunt Sarah. "How would you girls like to baste them in place?"

Once more the girls set to work, their slender fingers flying fast.

"Isn't it fun to work this way?" said Mildred.

"Many hands make light work," replied Mrs. Bobbsey. "I feel sure that we will get all the playsuits finished this afternoon."

Piece by piece the various parts of the garments were put together, until nothing remained to be done but the buttons and buttonholes.

It was wonderful how quickly those little pearl buttons went down the backs of the playsuits and, with the two mothers' help, dozens of buttonholes to go with them.

"I believe I could make playsuits all alone now," laughed Nan.

"Well, here's a pattern," spoke up Freddie, who had cut up a dozen newspapers trying to imitate Aunt Sarah's pattern.

"It looks like an elephant," giggled Flossie, who had been busy with her spools all afternoon.

It was only half-past four when Nan rang the bell to dismiss the sewing class. Everyone went downstairs for cookies and milk.

"We've had a lovely time," said Mabel, as she was leaving. "I'd love to come again and help with the sewing."

"Well, you are welcome to come, all of you," said Aunt Sarah. "We will make pyjamas for the boys next time. Now let's fold up the playsuits," she suggested. "Don't they look pretty?"

"When can we take them to the girls?" asked Flossie, eager to deliver the gifts to the camp children as soon as possible.

"Tomorrow afternoon," replied her mother. "The boys are going to pick vegetables for them in the morning, and we will drive over in the afternoon."

Uncle Daniel had given the boys permission to pick all the butter beans and string beans that were ripe, besides several baskets of spinach and other greens, and fruit.

"I guess we can get it all into the station wagon," laughed Bert, as he began to count up the baskets.

There were two of beans, three of greens, one of potatoes, two of sweet apples, besides five bunches of Freddie's radishes.

"Be sure to bring Sandy back with you," called Freddie, who was not going to the camp this time.

Nan and Aunt Sarah went with the boys, but how disappointed they were to find a new director in charge of the camp, and Sandy's eyes red from crying for Mrs. Manily.

"She went away and left me!" he sobbed. "Now I've lost two mummies!"

"Mrs. Manily has been called away by illness in her family," explained the new director, Mrs. Towne, "and I can't do anything with Sandy."

"Maybe if we take him over to our house for a few days, he will be happier," said Aunt Sarah. "He's very fond of our Freddie."

"Yes, Mrs. Manily spoke of that," said Mrs. Towne. "She received permission from the Society to let Sandy pay a visit to Mrs. Daniel Bobbsey. See, here is the card."

"Oh, that will be lovely!" cried Nan, hugging Sandy as tightly as her arms could squeeze. "Freddie told us to be sure to bring you back with us. Can I help you pack some clothes?"

"That would be very nice," said Mrs. Towne. "He'll take you to his tent."

While Nan and Sandy were gone, Aunt Sarah showed the director the vegetables in the car. Her eyes opened wide in surprise.

"How very wonderful!" she exclaimed. "Enough for my children for a week!"

She called several eight-year-old boys and asked them to carry the baskets of food to the kitchen tent. A few minutes later, when Nan returned with Sandy and his little suitcase, Aunt Sarah handed the package of playsuits to Mrs. Towne.

"Nan and her friends made these," she said, smiling at her niece.

When the director opened the package, she gasped. Neatly piled up were a dozen playsuits of various sizes.

"You—made these—for us!" cried Mrs. Towne. "They're lovely! Why, you must have spent hours and hours on them!"

Several little girls in the camp came running up, each hoping to receive one of the pretty blue-and-white gingham playsuits with the white organdy frills.

Aunt Sarah said she and Nan and Sandy must go now. Nan asked if she might take a minute to find Connie. Mrs. Towne shook her head sadly.

"Connie is ill," she said. "We have her in the hospital tent. The poor child ran too hard and collapsed. She is asleep now, and I don't think we had better disturb her."

Nan felt very bad about Connie. If she could only do something for her!

Sandy climbed into the front seat of the station wagon, promising Mrs. Towne he would be a very good boy while visiting at Meadow Brook Farm. Aunt Sarah stepped in behind the wheel, and Nan squeezed into the front seat with them.

"Good-bye, good-bye!" Sandy called to the other children, who watched for a minute, then went off to play.

When Freddie Bobbsey heard the station wagon roll into the driveway, he raced out of the barn, where he had been watching two carpenters repairing the damage caused by the fire.

"Hurrah! Hurrah!" he shouted. "I knew you would come, Sandy!"

The next minute Sandy was out of the car, and the two little boys ran off hand in hand to see Frisky, Snoop, the chickens, ducks, pigeons, and everything else.

Sandy was a city boy and knew nothing about country life, so that everything seemed wonderful to him, especially the chickens and ducks.

Snoop and Fluffy were put through their circus

tricks for the little boy's benefit, and then Freddie let Sandy play on his trapeze up under the apple tree. He showed him all the different kinds of turns Bert and Harry had taught the younger twin to perform on the swing.

"How long can you stay?" Freddie asked Sandy, while they were swinging.

"I don't know," Sandy replied vaguely. "I don't 'specially belong to anybody now," he added wistfully. "Mrs. Manily has gone away, you know, and I don't b'lieve in the new lady, do you?"

Freddie did not quite understand what Sandy meant, but he said "no" just to agree with him.

"And you know the big girl, Connie, who always helped me, she's sick, so I guess I can make-believe I'm your brother," continued Sandy.

"Course you can!" spoke up Freddie manfully, throwing his arms around his new playmate. "You're my twin brother, 'cause that's the realest kind. Now we are all twins—Nan and Bert, and Flossie and me and you!"

By this time the other Bobbseys had come out to welcome Sandy. They had thought it best to let Freddie entertain him first, so that he would not feel strange.

But now Uncle Daniel took the little fellow up

in his arms and into his heart, for all good men like Uncle Daniel love boys, especially when they are such manly little boys as Sandy and Freddie.

"He's my twin brother now, Uncle Daniel," Freddie announced. "Don't you think he's just like me?"

"He is certainly a fine little chap!" his uncle replied, "and he is quite like you at that, with his big smile. Now let us feed the chickens."

The hens were almost ready to eat the pearl buttons off Sandy's coat, so eager were they for their meal, and it was great fun for the two little boys to toss corn to them.

"Granny will eat from your hand," said Uncle Daniel. "You see, she is just like granite-grey stone, but we call her Granny for short."

The big Plymouth Rock hen came up to Sandy, and much to the little boy's delight ate the corn right out of his hand.

"Oh, she's a petting chicken!" he said, stroking Granny as he would a kitten. He sat down on the floor of the hen-house and let Granny come up on his lap.

There was so much feeding to do on the farm that before they knew how late it was, Martha appeared at the back door and rang the big dinner bell in a way that meant:

"Hurry up! Something will get cold if you don't!"

The "something" proved to be chicken pot pie with dumplings—the kind of dumplings of which everyone wants a second helping. And after that came apple pudding with hard sauce, just full of creamy butter.

"Is this a party?" Sandy whispered to Freddie, for he was not accustomed to more than cereal and milk at his evening meal.

"Yes, I guess so," ventured Freddie. "It's because you came."

After supper Bert played some records and the gay dance music made Sandy even more happy. He skipped around the room until the twins' mother said:

"All little folks should be in bed."

It had been a very exciting day for Sandy, and he was growing very sleepy. So was Freddie, with whom Sandy was to sleep. In spite of so many things to tell each other, the two little fellows fell asleep almost at once.

Mrs. Bobbsey came up and looked in the door. Two little blond heads so close together! She tucked the boys in a bit, and closed the hall door.

The big grandfather clock had just struck midnight, when Sandy awoke.

"Oh, what's that?" he asked himself.

There was something strange going on in the Bobbsey farm-house. Sandy woke Freddie.

"L-l-listen!" he whispered, his teeth chattering in fright.

The next instant both little boys put their heads under the covers.

CHAPTER XIX

A MIDNIGHT SCARE

EVERYBODY in the house was awake now. What was that strange noise?

"It's the piano again!" Bert whispered to Harry. "The ghost player!"

Sure enough, a nocturnal solo was coming up in queer snatches from the living-room.

Uncle Daniel was starting down the front stairs now.

"There it is again," whispered Bert, as another group of wild trills followed a thump on the keyboard. "Let's go down!"

The two boys reached the first floor right behind Harry's father. They turned on all the lights. As before, no one was there.

"It must have been one of the cats," Uncle Daniel declared. "Where are Snoop and Fluffy?" he asked.

The boys found the hall door to the cellar

partly open. There was Snoop on his cushion and Fluffy on hers.

"Funny," said Uncle Daniel, puzzled.

He lighted the piano lamp, which gave a strong light, but still there was no explanation of the mysterious playing.

"It certainly was the piano," he said.

All this time the people upstairs waited anxiously. Flossie held Nan so tightly about the neck that her elder sister could hardly breathe. Freddie and Sandy were still under the bedclothes, while Mrs. Bobbsey and Aunt Sarah listened in the hall.

"That sure is a ghost," whispered Dinah to Martha in the hall above. "Ghosts always love music," and her big eyes rolled expressively.

After a lapse of some minutes, Uncle Daniel remarked to the boys, "Well, I don't see that we can do any good by staying around here. We may as well put out the lights and get into bed again."

"But I cannot imagine what it could be!" Mrs. Bobbsey insisted, as he and the boys came upstairs.

"Neither can we!" agreed Uncle Daniel. "I have a suggestion to make. If we hear the noise again, everyone keep quiet and I'll sneak down alone in the darkness. Then maybe I can surprise whatever is making the music."

Everyone got back into bed, except Freddie and

Sandy, who had never left theirs. No sooner were the lights out and the household quiet than the piano sounded again.

"I'll surely get it this time, whatever it is!" Uncle Daniel whispered to Aunt Sarah.

He started downstairs in the dark without making a sound, while the piano kept on playing in discordant notes, the same as it had before.

Once in the living-room, Uncle Daniel pressed the light switch quickly, and the music ceased abruptly.

"There he is," he called, loud enough to be heard upstairs, and Flossie thought she surely would die of fright.

Slam! went a music book at something, and Sandy almost choked with fear.

Bang! went something else, that brought Bert and Harry downstairs to help catch the burglar.

"There he is in the corner!" called Uncle Daniel to the boys.

There began such a slam-banging that upstairs the rest of the family were in terror lest the burglar harm Harry and Bert and Uncle Daniel.

"We've got him!" cried Harry.

"Is he dead?"

"As a doornail!"

"What *is* it?" called Mrs. Bobbsey, almost as frightened as the children.

"A big fat mouse," replied Uncle Daniel, chuckling, "and your Snoop was chasing her!"

Flossie came down to stroke Snoop and tell him he had tried hard to catch the mouse, and not to feel bad about not getting it.

"In the morning I'll give you an extra special breakfast for a reward," she promised.

It was some time before everybody was quieted down again, but finally the midnight scare was over and the Bobbseys turned to dreams of the happy summer-time they were enjoying.

Two days later, when Uncle Daniel came up from the post office, he brought a note from Mrs. Manily, who had returned to the fresh air camp. He told Nan what it said, and she went to find her twin.

"Sandy has to go back!" she whispered to Bert. "His father has sent for him, but Mother says not to say anything to Sandy or Freddie—they might worry. Aunt Sarah will drive Sandy back to the camp and Mrs. Manily will break the news to him. I'm so sorry he has to go back to the city."

"So am I," Bert answered. "I don't see why they can't leave him here when he is so happy."

"But it's his own father, you know, and something was said about a rich aunt. Maybe she is going to adopt Sandy."

At that moment Sandy came running along

the path with Freddie. Mrs. Bobbsey called the children to her.

"We are going over to see Mrs. Manily today, Sandy," she said. "Won't you be awfully glad to see her again?"

"Uh-huh," he faltered, getting a tighter hold on Freddie's hand, "but I want to come back here," he said, almost pleadingly.

So many changes in the poor little boy's life had made him fear still another uprooting.

"Oh, I am sure you will come to see us again," Mrs. Bobbsey said kindly. "Maybe you can visit us in Lakeport when we go home in the fall."

Freddie insisted upon going to the camp with Sandy, "to make sure he would come again."

It was only the happiness of seeing his daddy once more that kept Sandy from crying when they told him he was to go home. Even the thought of a ride on a great big fast train did not help much.

"You see," Mrs. Manily explained to Mrs. Bobbsey, "a wealthy aunt of Edward's suddenly has decided that she wants to adopt him, so we will have to give him up, I am afraid. How I shall miss him!"

"I'm afraid Freddie is going to be heart-broken," said the twins' mother.

Freddie kissed Sandy good-bye. It was not the kind of a caress that girls give each other. The two little fellows said good-bye, kissed each other very quickly, then looked down at the ground in a brave effort not to cry.

Mrs. Bobbsey gave Sandy a real mother's kiss, and he said, "Oh, I'm coming to see you as soon as everybody lets me!"

So Sandy started off to another home, where his father felt sure he would find the love and protection that he deserved.

Before going to bed, the twins heard that the old well was going to be cleaned the next afternoon.

"How do they do that?" asked Freddie excitedly.

"Wait and see," said Uncle Daniel. "That old well will be full of surprises."

CHAPTER XX

WHAT THE WELL CONTAINED

WHEN the twins came down to breakfast the next morning, what a nice surprise awaited them! Daddy Bobbsey had arrived unexpectedly, late the night before.

"Oh, Daddy, you can see us clean the well!" exclaimed Freddie.

"Freddie means the men," said Flossie, giving her father a hug.

"And what's my little Fat Fairy been doing while I was away?" he asked.

"I grew carrots," Flossie answered.

"They grew themselves," scoffed Freddie.

Mr. Bobbsey laughed. He decided to look at them anyway, and also at Nan's garden, which she had tended faithfully for nearly four weeks. As soon as breakfast was over, the girls took him up to their very own private vegetable patch.

"Why, I declare!" Mr. Bobbsey exclaimed in

real surprise. "You have done splendidly. This is a very fine garden."

Mrs. Bobbsey and Aunt Sarah had come along too, as they had not seen the garden for two weeks. They also were amazed at the result of Nan's and Flossie's work.

"See my carrots!" cried Flossie proudly. "They're tall enough now to pick."

Before anyone could stop her, she pulled up a whole handful of the fuzzy green leaves with slender orange carrots hanging from them.

"They grew! They grew!" Flossie shouted, dancing around in delight.

"You must only pull the big ones," her father told her. "And did you really plant them?"

"Yes! John showed me," she declared, and Nan said that was really Flossie's contribution to the garden.

"Now I'd suggest," Aunt Sarah remarked, "that we let our girl farmers pick their vegetables for dinner, and then we all will be able to sample them."

At this the girls started in to pick the very biggest heads of lettuce, and Flossie looked carefully to get the very largest carrots in the patch. Finally, enough were gathered, and the vegetables were carried down to the kitchen.

"You must prepare them yourselves for the

table," the twins' mother said. "Let us see what a pretty dish you can make."

Scraping carrots was not an easy task for Nan and Flossie, but when at last Nan brought the dish in to the dinner table, everybody said how pretty it looked.

"Nan, you serve the salad," Aunt Sarah said, and Nan very neatly put a few crisp lettuce leaves on each small plate, and on the top she placed a few strips of carrots, then poured dressing over each one.

"Just think," remarked Aunt Sarah, "you've done it all from the garden to the table!"

Nan and Flossie smiled, justly proud of their success as gardeners.

"I have another surprise," said Nan.

She got up and went to the pantry. In a moment she returned with a dish of delicious-looking chocolate candy.

"Do you remember when Aunt Sarah wrote that she was going to show me how to make this?" Nan asked with a smile, looking sideways at her twin.

"Oh, boy!" said Bert. "Hurry up and pass it around!"

Aunt Sarah suggested that the candy be saved until after dessert, so the children had to wait, but all during the meal longing eyes were cast toward the dish which Aunt Sarah kept in front of her.

At last, however, the candy was passed. It was so good that everyone had two pieces and Bert begged his sister not to forget how to make it. He wanted some more as soon as they got home.

Finally, Aunt Sarah arose from the table, and the family walked outdoors. The grown-ups as well as the children were eager to watch the men clean the well.

The one to be cleaned was an old landmark, which had been at the corner of the road and the lane for a hundred years. Many passers-by enjoyed stopping at it for a good cold drink, but for a couple of weeks now it had been closed because the water had not tasted good. Evidently something unpleasant-tasting had fallen inside. Just what it was remained a mystery. But the mystery would soon be solved.

"Here come the men," called Bert, as two well cleaners arrived in a truck.

They wore oilskin jackets and hip boots. In the truck were a windlass, a suction pump, broom, brushes, and various tools.

All the neighbourhood boys had gathered—all interested in the work because at one time or another they had lost articles in the water. Maybe they would get them back!

Freddie pushed his way through. "Now keep back," ordered Nan. "You can see just as well from this big stone, and you will not be in any danger here."

So Freddie and Flossie mounted the rock while the other boys moved up closer to the well.

First the men removed the well shelter—the wooden house that covered the opening. Then they took a long rope with a weight on the end and let it down into the water.

"They want to see how deep it is," Nan explained to the small twins.

The rope was pulled up and the wet part measured. "Plenty of water down there," one of the men said. "Well, let's get the pump going."

A long hose was lowered into the water. Then the men worked the hand pump on the end of it. Soon a strong stream of water was gushing on to the road. It was several minutes before the stream began to lessen, but finally it became only a trickle.

"Now they're ready to go down," said Nan.

The open well was covered with a wooden platform in the centre of which was a large round hole. Over this the windlass was set up and a bucket and rope attached. One of the men stepped into the bucket, a flashlight and a sack in his hand.

"Oh!" cried Flossie. "Is he going to ride down into the well?"

"Yes, he is," Nan replied.

"He's a diver like in my picture-book," said Freddie.

"He is one kind of a diver," Nan laughed, "only he doesn't have to wear a funny suit with air pipes in it like the ones ocean divers wear."

It took several seconds for the man, whose name was Dick, to reach the bottom of the well, because he went slowly.

"Now Dick can see stars in the sky," said Harry to Flossie and Freddie.

"But there are no stars in the sky," Freddie contradicted, looking up at the clear blue sky of the fine summer day.

"Oh, yes there are," laughed the man at the well. "Lots of them, too, but you can only see them in the dark, and it's good and dark down in that deep well."

This seemed very strange, but of course it was true. And the well cleaner told them, if they didn't believe it, to look up a fireplace chimney some day, and they might be able to see the same strange sight. Leaning over, he called down to Dick:

"Have you solved the mystery yet?"

"Sure have," the other answered. "A crate of cabbage fell in here. That's what's been spoiling the water. I'll send it up."

So the first load to be sent up in the bucket was the crate of cabbage. Flossie was glad it was carried off into a field right away, "'Cause it smells awful!" she said.

Once more the bucket was lowered. When it came up again and the contents were examined, what a roar of laughter went up! The first thing the well man held up was a dripping, scraggly, grey wig! Then he showed a tin horn.

"They're from our Hallowe'en party last fall!" cried Harry. "Mildred was an old witch. Somebody pulled her wig off and threw it, and nobody could find it."

The man dumped the rest of the contents on the ground. Harry jumped forward.

"Hurrah! My lost baseball!" he exclaimed, yanking out the soggy, discoloured ball which had been knocked far and lost during a game.

"And my cap pistol," called Tom Mason, as the rusty object was extracted from the pile.

"Oh, there's my sister Nettie's doll!" exclaimed Ned Prentice. "August and I were playing toss with the doll and let it fly in the well."

"I'm sure Nettie will be glad to get it back," said Nan. "It's a good doll."

"She's never had another since I lost it," said Ned, glad to be able to return it to his sister.

Fortunately the doll was waterproof and had hardly been injured by its long soaking in the well.

The next thing pulled out was a big pipe with a long curved stem.

"That belongs to Hans Bruen," declared Jack Hopkins. "I remember the night he dropped it."

"Foolish Hans—to try to drink with a pipe like that in his mouth!" laughed the well cleaner.

The big bucket was lowered twice more and all sorts of articles were brought up; a dozen tin cups, two milk pails, a saucepan, two felt hats, and even an old slipper!

"Seems as if folks can't hold on to things when they get near a well," the man grinned.

Finally Dick gave a signal that he was ready to come up, and soon the windlass was groaning and straining. In a few minutes he was at the top.

"Look at this!" he said to the onlookers, holding up a beautiful gold watch. "Ever hear of anyone losing a watch in the well?"

"Are there any initials on it?" Harry asked. "Mr. Peter Burns lost one."

The well cleaner looked. Engraved on the back of the old-fashioned watch were the initials P.B.

"Oh, it must be his!" exclaimed Harry. "I'll take it to him. Say, you didn't find a gold wedding ring, did you? Mrs. Burns lost it at the same time he dropped the watch in."

"Here it is," chuckled the well cleaner, and he handed the gold band to Harry.

Everyone knew the old Burns couple would be delighted to have their jewellery back. They were among the best-liked farmers around Meadow Brook, and their neighbours were very sorry about the many misfortunes they had had.

"And I have one last prize," said Dick. "Who's going to claim this?"

He held up a pearl necklace. Nan Bobbsey gasped and sprang forward.

CHAPTER XXI

THE GOOD-BYE PARTY

"MY BEADS! My lost beads!" cried Nan. "Oh, how glad I am that you found them!"

She took the necklace and examined it carefully. Yes, the clasp identified them. The beads were a bit dirty, but otherwise as good as ever.

"I thought I would never see them again," said Nan. "I must tell Mother!" And she started for the house with flying feet.

Mrs. Bobbsey was very glad to learn that the lovely Christmas gift from Uncle William and Aunt Emily had been found, and declared that Nan was certainly a lucky girl to get it back.

"I'm especially glad that it was found right now," said Mrs. Bobbsey, "because Aunt Emily may ask you about the necklace."

Nan looked puzzled. "What do you mean, Mother?"

Mrs. Bobbsey's eyes twinkled. "I've just been talking on the phone to Ocean Cliff."

"Aunt Emily Minturn?" Nan asked.

Her mother nodded. "She is inviting all of us to spend part of August with her and Uncle William."

"Oh, how wonderful!" cried Nan. "Are we going?"

Mrs. Bobbsey said she had told her sister Emily they would be leaving the farm in a couple of days, and would like to go to the seaside for a visit.

"May I tell the others?" Nan requested excitedly.

"If you like," her mother smiled.

Nan ran all the way back to the well, where the children were watching the men load up their gear into the truck. Dick was saying:

"You've got fine pure water now. The well's scrubbed, and there's nothing in the water but two little lizards. They'll eat up all the bugs that get in the water."

"That's right," said the other man. "They'll keep it clean."

The children waved good-bye, then Nan made her big announcement.

"You're going to the seaside!" cried Mildred. "I wish I were."

"You mean it, Sis?" exclaimed Bert. "Gee, that's swell!"

"Oh, I just love the seaside," said Flossie. "'Cept when the waves knock me down."

The Meadow Brook children wanted to hear more about Ocean Cliff.

"Another aunt and uncle of ours live there," Nan explained, "and a cousin, too. Her name is Dorothy. She has two little donkeys and a cart to go riding in on the beach."

"I'm going to drive them," announced Freddie.

"Better look out," Harry warned him. "Donkeys like to kick."

"Oh, I can manage 'em," Freddie boasted. "And I can catch crabs, too."

"I'd like to see you," said Flossie; a bit disgusted with her twin's bragging.

The children talked for a long time about the seaside, but finally Nan declared that they could not possibly have a better time there than they had had at Meadow Brook Farm.

"I wish you were going with us," Bert said to Harry. "There's no boy at the Minturns'—just Dorothy. I'll have to find someone new to play with."

Later; Nan told her twin that maybe Harry could come down and visit them. Even if Aunt Emily was not Harry's aunt, maybe she would invite him.

"I hope so," said Bert.

Next morning Aunt Sarah appeared in a suit she often wore when she was going to town.

"Well, my dears," she said to the twins, "you are leaving for Ocean Cliff tomorrow, so I want you to invite all your Meadow Brook friends to a little party this afternoon. I'm going down to the village to order some things for it. We'll make it just the best party ever."

The children were thrilled and went at once to invite their friends; some by telephone, others by notes delivered by Harry and Bert, who rode to the various farm-houses on their bicycles. Everyone accepted.

As they were returning home, the boys met Mark Teron coming along on his bicycle. They were merely going to nod to him and ride on, but he stopped them.

"Say, you're just the fellows I want to see," he said.

"Yes? What for?" Harry asked.

"I—I want to thank you for not squealing to my father about the fire," Mark said, embarrassed. "Pop would really let me have it if he knew.

"And listen, Bert," Mark added—he paused a moment as if it was hard for him to go on—"I think you're the best city boy I ever met. I'm sorry I was mean to you."

Bert was embarrassed, but he quickly accepted the apology. "That's all right, Mark," he said. "City boys aren't very sharp in the country. I'm glad you think I made the grade."

On the spur of the moment Bert invited Mark to come to the party. Mark seemed very pleased and said he would like to come.

"Three o'clock," Harry called as they rode off.

Back at Meadow Brook Farm the other children were busy having last-minute fun.

"John's going to send me a great big pumpkin," Freddie announced. He was bringing some vegetables to the kitchen in his express wagon. "I saw the baby pumpkin in the cornfield. By Hallowe'en he'll be a big man."

At three o'clock the Bobbsey children, wearing their best clothes, came outside to greet their guests. Mildred Manners was the first to arrive.

"I hope you'll come again next year," she said. "We've had such a lovely time with you this summer. And, Nan, I brought you this little handkerchief to remember me by."

The handkerchief was made of linen and had a big N embroidered in the corner. Nan was delighted with the gift, and hugged Mildred.

"Here is something to remember *me* by," said Mabel Herold, handing Nan a snapshot album, and receiving a kiss in return.

And Nettie brought, of all things, a little live duck for Freddie! It was just like a lump of cotton-wool, it was so soft and fluffy.

"We'll fatten him up for Christmas," laughed Bert, joking.

"No, you won't!" snapped Freddie. "I am going to have a little house for him and a lake, and a boat——"

"Are you going to teach him to row?" teased Harry.

"Well, he can swim better than—than——"

"I can," said August Stout, recalling the day he had fallen into the water while fishing.

After games had been played, and ice-cream and cake had been served on the lawn, Aunt Sarah brought out a big, round white paper pie. She placed it on a table, and drew out several long white ribbons that were folded over the top. On each ribbon was pinned the name of one of the guests.

"Now this is your Jack Horner pie," said Aunt Sarah, "and when you put in your thumb, you will pull out a plum!"

Nan read off the names, and each girl and boy took the place assigned in the circle. Finally, everybody was clutching a ribbon in his hand.

"Nettie has number one," said Nan. "You pull first, Nettie."

Nettie jerked her ribbon and out from the pie came a dear little toy piano. It was made of paper, of course, and so very small it could stand on Nettie's hand.

"Give us a tune!" laughed Harry, as Nettie discovered it really was a little box of candy.

"Mildred next," announced Nan.

On the end of Mildred's ribbon was a comic book. This caused a laugh, for Mildred was very fond of comics.

Mabel got a hobbyhorse—because she was learning to ride horseback. And Nan received a miniature sewing machine, to remind her of her fresh air work.

Of course Tom Mason got a horse—a colt it really was, kicking its hind hoofs into the air. And Jack Hopkins' gift was a wheelbarrow. Harry pulled out a boat, and Bert got a cider barrel.

They were all favours, filled with candy, and the children giggled as they pretended to make them work.

"Freddie, we are going to let you and Flossie put your thumbs in the pie," said Aunt Sarah, "and whoever gets the prize will be the real Jack Horner."

All but the centre of the pie was gone now, and into this Flossie put her thumb. She fished around hard, and brought out a little gold ring.

"Oh, isn't it sweet!" all the girls exclaimed.

Then Freddie had his turn. "Can't I put in two fingers?" he pleaded.

"No, only one!" his mother insisted.

After careful preparation Freddie put in his thumb and pulled out a big candy plum!

"Open it!" called Nan.

The plum was put together in halves, and when Freddie opened it he found a real watch.

"It's going!" he cried. "And I can tell time!" declared the happy boy, for he had been learning every single minute on Martha's clock in the kitchen.

The party was over. The children said good-bye. Besides the play favours, each one carried away a lasting gift, that of friendship for the Bobbsey twins.

"Good-bye!" was the answering cry, and then the visitors left in a crowd, waving their hands as they disappeared in the cars that had brought them.

"What a perfectly lovely time we have had here!" declared Nan to Bert. "We must thank Aunt Sarah and Uncle Daniel."

"Oh, the country can't be beat!" answered her twin brother. "Still, I'll be glad to get to the seaside, won't you. It's getting awfully hot, and a good old swim will be swell."

"Hurrah for the seaside!" yelled Freddie.

They all went into the house to get ready for the trip.

Read more of the Twins' adventures in
"THE BOBBSEY TWINS"